INFINITE SECRETS

PROLOGUE

"Yo, my balls feel heavy. I mean, hey big of course but they normally don't feel like this! Come look at this, Chantel," Noah called out.

"Noah, I am not about to come look at your balls," I grunted, rolling my eyes.

"You look at nigga's balls all day, but you can't look at mine?" Noah questioned, annoyed that I wouldn't come in the bathroom.

"I do not look at balls all day, Noah. Yes, I'm a nurse that works in a sperm bank, but my day does not consist of me checking out balls all day," I yelled back.

"For real, I think my shit's swollen. I swear Alana hoe ass better not have given me nothing. I ain't never heard of heavy ball disease, that must be some new 2030 STD. Seriously, I'm not playing. It hurts. Can you come look?" Noah whimpered.

"Aughhh! Yes, Noah. You better not be playing either," I warned.

Easing open the bathroom door, I quickly stepped inside shutting the door behind me. Instantly, I felt guilty for being this close to my sister's boyfriend. Everyone knew there was no Noah Roberts without Alana Man. Noah and I had become best friends because he always used to take up for me when Alana would treat me badly. I'm four years younger than Alana, so I always wanted to follow her around and copy everything she did. You know, regular little sister shenanigans. Alana hates how close Noah and I are, but it is what it is. She swears I have a crush on him, but I just see him as my brother —nothing more, nothing less.

"Are you going to take off your towel or not?"

"Never mind, this shit's weird."

"Noah, if you really think something is wrong, let me see."

"Okay."

We both stood there in silence not wanting to be the one to make the first move. I moved forward to take control of the situation. Hell, I'm a nurse, and I have seen enough private parts to last me a lifetime.

I yanked the towel from around his waist. Just wanting to get it over with.

"Hey, be gentle with me! Shit, no wonder you don't have a man with your rough ass! You probably scare them all away!" Noah barked.

"You want my help or not?" I countered.

"Yeah, man," he responded gingerly.

I decided to sit on the toilet, so I didn't have to bend down or get on my knees to inspect his genitals. Even though I was at his house in the bathroom, I wanted to remain as professional as possible.

"Noah, come over here so I can see," I demanded.

I closed my eyes as Noah began to do the duck walk towards me. He was trying to cover himself but needed me to check it at the same time. This dude was too funny.

Now standing in front of me with his eyes facing the ceiling, Noah asked if I needed him to cough and hold his balls.

"Noah, if you're holding them, how am I going to see if they are enlarged?"

"Shit, sis, I don't know. Let's just get this over with. I feel embarrassed," he croaked.

Looking at his penis lay passively against his leg unexcited, for a lack of better words, I understood why Alana had to fight so many girls in high school and even some in college. If he was hanging this low and thick without being aroused, I didn't even want to imagine what his full potential was.

"How does this feel? Does it hurt?" I asked him after I poked around on his balls. He was correct; one was noticeably larger than the other, and instantly, I felt something off. It felt like a tumor, but I wanted to ask a few questions before I got too alarmed.

"Noah, where's Chantel? I saw her car out front and her purse on the couch," Alana inquired, busting into the bathroom.

Noah turned around so quick his dick hit me in the forehead. I screamed.

"All the hoes, I had to fight over you and you messing with my sister?" Alana yelled.

"Lana, this is not what it looks like!" I jumped up to defend myself.

"Fuck you, Chantel! I hate you! I never want to speak to you again!" Alana screamed while stomping out of the bathroom.

Noah stood there frozen, his hands covering his private area as if she had never seen it before.

"Alana, he was embarrassed but said he had unusual swelling and finally asked me to check it out. He's right; it feels like a tumor in his right testicle. It is not what it looked like; I promise. Neither of us would ever do that to you," I reassured.

"Bitch, fuck you and him! The eyes don't lie! I know what I walked into; you were sucking his dick! Everyone always said it wasn't normal for y'all to be that close. I've always took up for y'all, swearing no matter what, y'all would never do that to me," Alana screamed, swinging on me.

"Alana, I understand you're upset at what you think you saw. But if you swing on me again, I will knock your ass out. I mean that!" I shouted back, holding her hands at her wrist.

Noah came around the corner with just his towel tied back around his waist. Alana started wrestling with me to get loose from my grasp. As soon as their eyes locked, she broke down crying, snot flying everywhere. I loosened my grip, allowing her to break free from my grip.

"Lana, baby, I swear it's not what it looked like. I'd never do that disrespectful shit to you. I love Chantel like my own little sister. You know that. Honestly, even having her look at me naked grossed me out. But my shit is swollen and feels heavy and weird. She's a professional. I trust her. I went about it wrong; I should have told you first then asked her to check it in your presence. Or called a doctor, but baby, she was here when I noticed it got bigger than before," Noah confessed.

"Alana, you are my sister, and I'd never touch any man you dealt with sexually. That's nasty as hell. And especially not Noah. He is my brother. Period," I stated.

"Nah, y'all gaming me right now. I'm getting out of here!" Alana shouted, brushing past me.

"Alana, he's going to need you!" I urged.

Alana plucked her purse from the couch, angrily stabbing her shoe with her foot, trying to get them on quickly. She was ignoring both of our pleas, humming lowly under her breath. Noah confiscated her keys from her, so she'd have to hear us out. In true Alana fashion, that didn't stop her from rushing out the door.

I stepped in the hallway behind her as she raced down the steps, I yelled, "Alana, I think it's cancer!"

"What?" she asked, shocked.

Alana stopped dead in her tracks in the middle of the stairs. She looked torn on if she wanted to believe me or not.

"You're lying," she accused softly.

"We won't know for sure until he sees the doctor, but I'm going to call a doctor I know first thing in the morning to get him an urgent appointment," I explained.

"I can't deal with this!" Alana cried as she turned to run down the rest of the stairs, never looking back.

"Cancer?" Noah repeated, standing there in his towel with a baffled look on his face.

Chapter One

CHANTEL

One Year Later

All Hell Breaks Loose

I snuck into the medical supplies room to get a breather. Today had been a trying day, and I still had two hours before the end of my shift. I wish I could blink twice, and it'd be quitting time.

"There you are! Oh, thank God I found you! I messed up so bad, it's been crazy, and I'm frazzled," our new nurse, Pamela, said.

"What happened? I'm sure it can be fixed. I'll help you," I offered.

Pamela burst into tears wildly shaking her head.

Her body shook as she stumbled over the next words to leave her mouth.

"Yesterday, I sent the wrong sperm to Mrs. Gianna Wesley. Donor 1058 instead of Donor 1053. It's so hard to make out Dr. Hahn's handwriting. I typed in the wrong information to send over to her In-Vitro lab. I had it sent out yesterday, I tried to stop it this afternoon when I went to confirm that everything was correct and made it. She was already off the table; her appointment was first thing this morning. I don't know what to do, I'm going to be fired and possibly sued for this shit!" Pamela cried.

Pamela bawled so hard her whole body shook as she began to dry-heave. I snaked my arms around Pamela to wrap her in a tight embrace to calm her down. We both knew the outcome of her fate was termination. This was considered a non-negotiable offense since the company could be sued for millions of dollars. Her confession replayed in my mind, I felt so sorry for her. Dr. Hahn's handwriting was always difficult to read. The donor number flashed into my head again. Instantly, I stiffened. Yanking my body away from her, I stared deep into her eyes praying I didn't hear her correctly.

"Pam, what donor did you say?" I asked, my voice full of panic.

"Ummm, donor 1058," she answered with a sniffle.

My shoulders drooped, a sheen of sweat coated my forehead. I felt my eyes roll back in my head as I suddenly became dizzy. My heart dropped to the soles of my feet. My body swayed as my knees buckled.

"Chantel! Are you okay?" Pamela screeched, grabbing me by the shoulders to steady me.

I opened my mouth to speak, but my jaw snapped back shut as quickly as my lips parted. The words wouldn't come as my tongue suddenly became heavy. Swallowing the scream in my throat, I let the tears flow down my cheeks uninterrupted.

"Please talk to me Chantel, I know I messed up, but it's something you aren't explaining to me," Pamela pressed.

As my heart thumped wildly, I drew my next breath so deep, it caused my lungs to burn. I closed my eyes to calm my nerves before answering her question.

"Donor 1058 is my brother. Well, my brother in-law. Last year he was diagnosed with non-seminoma testicular cancer. He didn't want to take the chance of not being able to be a father in the future, so he preserved his sperm before the radiation and chemotherapy treatments started," I cried quietly.

"You have to be shitting me! Oh my God, are you serious right now? Not only did I fuck up majorly, but I just changed the dynamics of your family? Chantel, you have to know it was an accident! I'm so, so sorry," she sobbed.

Finally, wiping tears from my now swollen eyes, I ushered her out of the supply room, promising that we'd figure out something to just keep it to herself for now. I knew we had been gone for a while, and someone would be looking for us soon if they weren't already. Squeezing my hand tightly in hers, Pamela solemnly shook her head, silently agreeing to let me try to deal with the mess she made.

The rest of the day raced by in a blur. I could barely focus on the clients I had because I was rehearsing in my head how to tell Noah and Alana someone else was walking around with his seed trying to attach to her uterus. My mind went back to the day we found out Noah indeed had cancer. We just couldn't wrap our minds around the thought of him not being in perfect health at the young age of twenty-five. Alana sat between us at the doctor's office, wailing like we were burying him that very moment. Part of me believes she was also crying because she treated us both so bad earlier that day and the days leading up to the appointment. She had always been a stubborn person. Even when the truth was evident, once she made up her mind, nothing else mattered. The moment I saw the sorrow reach her eyes, she hugged me tightly and apologized, thanking me for helping him catch this early. And just like that, all was forgiven and forgotten.

I texted Pamela to meet me in the parking garage at my car, so we could talk. Placing a request in the system for the day off for tomorrow, I shut down my computer after wishing my co-workers a good night. Gathering my personal belongings, I made my way out the building with the weight of the world on my shoulders. I didn't have the slightest idea of what to say to Pamela, let alone Noah and Alana. Their relationship had been unusually rocky lately, but I knew they'd bounce back stronger than ever as always. Now, I wasn't so sure. This would unequivocally break their hearts. I just hoped they would be able to move past this.

As we approached the front door, we could hear yelling

going on inside of the house. I couldn't quite make out what was being said, but it sounded one-sided. Pamela stood uncomfortably close behind me, fidgeting with the tassels on her purse as I rang the doorbell. We could hear the heavy footsteps stomping to the door in a rush. Noah yanked the door open so fast a rush of air smacked me in the face.

"Hey, No. I can tell this isn't a good time. Maybe we should come back?" I suggested.

"We who? Who is she?" he questioned with a scowl on his face.

Directing his attention back to me, Noah asked what was going on.

"We have something to tell you, it's major, but we can wait. Are y'all okay in here? Where is Alana? She hasn't stormed the door yet," I chuckled.

"She's in the bed sick. Come in so we can talk. Nothing you can say would be worse than the shit I found out today," he scoffed, opening the door wide so we could pass through.

"Take a seat at the table, let me shut the door to the bedroom," Noah offered.

"Noah, let's just talk about this!" Alana yelled weakly.

The sound of weakness in her voice made my skin prickle with goosebumps. I shot Pamela a look of confusion, jumping up from the table. I walked briskly back to the bedroom to see what was going on. Noah was already headed in my direction, so we passed each other in the hallway. Noah didn't even acknowledge me as I walked past him.

Slowly creeping open the door to the bedroom, I saw

Alana already half-sleep on the bed. I dropped to one knee in front of her, lightly touching her hand, asking her if she was okay.

"I fucked up. I really fucked up," she whispered.

"Did Noah hurt you? Best friend, brother in-law or not, you are my sister first! I'll kill him before I let something happen to you," I declared.

"He didn't do anything to me, I had an abortion today. Long story, but he found out, and of course, it wasn't his baby. I doubt he will stay with me after this. Yes, he's yelled and cursed me out after finding out, but he didn't put his hands on me. I'm tired and weak, come check on me tomorrow, and we can talk. I promise," she breathed.

Ripples of shock shot through my body; I know she didn't say what I thought she said. I couldn't command my legs to move out of my spot in front of the bed.

"Alana," I gasped.

"Chantel, not today. I promise to tell you everything once I feel a little better. Please," she pleaded with me to leave the room.

I leaned in, wiping a few strands of hair out of her face. I kissed her forehead, telling her that I loved her and walked out the room, shutting the door behind me softly. I made my way back into the dining room to only find it empty. Taking long strides towards the living room, I found Noah and Pamela in the living room facing each other on opposite couches, but they were sitting in awkward silence.

"She's back. What do you need to tell me?" Noah asked, sliding to the edge of his seat.

The hurt in his eyes made me want to wrap my arms around him, but the angry grimace on his face told me to talk to him about it in private.

"Noah, I know this has been a trying day. Maybe we should do this another time," I offered.

"Spit the shit out, one of you. Both of you, someone just better start talking," he spat.

"I accidentally sent your sperm to the wrong woman! I tried to fix my error, but she had already left the doctor's office. If everything goes well, she will be having your baby in nine months. I'm so sorry. I don't expect any special treatment because I am Chantel's friend, but I wanted to tell you myself and express my sincere apologies," Pamela blurted.

Noah snapped his head back, letting out a gut-wrenching scream. I leaped from my seat to console my best friend. He snatched me up from the floor, twirling me in his arms. Now laughing like a mad man. Abruptly, he put me down, signaling for Pamela to come to him. Nervously, she closed the distance between them. He grabbed her into a tight embrace, rocking her back and forth.

"I won't press charges or cause you to lose your job. I can't speak for the other party, however. If she is understanding and allows me to be in my child's life, we will be good. God makes no mistakes and we can't stop fate. After what I learned today, this just may have been what was next in my life. All I ask is that you get me the information of the woman that's carrying my seed. Oh, and you better pray she's not ugly. I'll love my seed, but I ain't trying to have no ugly ass babies running around here calling me daddy, embarrassing me and shit!" Noah concluded.

"I have the information right here for you. I put it in this envelope. Hold on, let me get my purse from the kitchen. Again, I know you are positively dealing with this right now, but I am so sorry. I will be more careful from here on out," Pamela apologized again.

After providing Noah with the information she printed out, Pamela made her way to the door. We both walked her out, I informed her I took off for tomorrow to help come up with a game plan about the baby and how to handle it. Pamela told us to call her if there was anything more that she could help with. No sooner than she cut her car on, I began bombarding Noah with questions about him and Alana.

Noah swiftly wiped his hand down his face. A look of frustration mixed with anger replaced the calm look that was just on his face.

"Your sister decided to do some grimy ass shit! I know I've fucked up plenty of times in the past. Hell, so has she, but I've never went in no bitch raw. Never. The fucked up part is if she didn't forget her purse in my car, I wouldn't have ever found out any of this," he snapped.

I reached out to take his hand in mine. I knew how much love they had between them. Even if the beginning and middle was a rough start, the love never left. Over the last year, after he was diagnosed with cancer, she stood tall in his corner, being there every step of the way.

"She left her purse in my car last night, and I left early this morning to go to Jared's before work. The piece of trash ass nigga she was fucking didn't go with her, nor did he show up. She called her little broke, groupie friend, Tina and she met her up there, but Tina didn't have the money to lend her. So, this dummy takes the card out of the glovebox that I leave in there for emergencies and paid for it. The alert popped up on my phone. Since I was busy at work, I didn't catch the alert until around lunchtime. I called the credit card company to report it as fraud and asked for more information on the charge. They were able to give me an address, so I went down there to see if I could find out who stole my card information. Low and behold, I see Tina helping Alana doped up ass to the car," he finished strained.

"Damn," I remarked.

"This is going to be hard to bounce back from," I said.

"It's no coming back from this shit. It's certain lines you don't cross. I'm going to stay with Jared tonight. You may want to stay here to keep an eye on your sister throughout the night. On another note, tomorrow I need you to go with me to find my baby momma. I'll call you in the morning when I'm ready to roll. I love you though, sis. Real talk," he spoke, kissing me on my cheek before bouncing off to his car.

Chapter Two

NOAH

My Brother, My Keeper

"Jared!" I screamed through the house, shutting the door behind me.

"I'm in the living room! And stop yelling in my damn house," he shouted back.

I sped up, swiftly crossing the open floor plan to reach my older brother. *Pop!* I smacked the hell out the back of his head. Before I could leap out of the way, he reached his arm up, snatching me by the collar, yanking me across the chair. We tumbled onto the floor, wrestling and play fighting as always. Out of breath, Jared was the first to give up.

"Yeah, the pretty boy gets tired quick, huh?" I taunted.

"Nigga, whatever. I was just tired of beating yo' ass," he huffed, still trying to catch his breath.

Flashing him the 'OK' sign, I extended my hand to help

him off the floor. Now on his feet, he grabbed me into a bro hug.

"What's up, little man?" he asked.

"Nigga, you the little man," I smirked, rolling my eyes.

The back and forth between my brother and I never stopped. It was all out of love, though. From the time I could walk, I've always looked up to him. He's been my best friend all my life. Since we were only two years apart, we did so much together. He had always been the best big brother anyone could ask for. We were lucky to have both of our loving parents' home with us, but I still looked up to my big brother more than my father. Jared had always been wild and flashy, doing whatever he felt, when he felt. My father was a dedicated, hardworking, loving, protective husband and father, but he was always quiet. My mother was outgoing, she slowed down majorly once we got a little older. I've heard plenty of stories of her younger days, and moms was about all the shits!

We separated, him taking his seat back on the black leather loveseat he was sitting on when I came in. I took a seat on the opposite couch, perched on the arm of it instead of relaxing into the cushions.

Jared swung his legs over the edge of the loveseat, getting comfortable waiting for me to spill whatever that was clearly on my mind. We stared at each other in silence. It was crazy how much we looked like twins even though he was older, and I was an inch taller than him. Many women compared our looks to the dude Boris Kodjoe. We were around the same color as him, with similar features. Jared even rocked a bald head like him, standing at 6', with muddy colored eyes, you could also tell he never missed a day in the gym because of his build. He kept his face as smooth as a baby's bottom. On the other hand, I was 6'1 with a connecting beard, low Caesar fade, and chestnut-brown colored eyes like our mother.

"Nigga, you gone say what the fuck on your mind or you gone stare at me all night? Shit, I know I'm fine and all, but we brothers and I don't go that way," he joked, snapping his fingers in the air flamboyantly.

"I can't tell," I delivered back smartly.

Jared gave me the finger, checking his phone as it chimed. After he answered his text message, I began spilling the events of my day to him.

"You'll never believe this shit, yo," I said, cradling my head in my hands.

He sat up, now sitting straight in the chair, tapping his bare foot against his cherry wood flooring.

"Alana's sneaky ass got pregnant by some nigga and got an abortion today," I reflected.

"Oh shit, that's fucked up, No! Fuck that hoe, you good? Want me to find that nigga? You know I got you, no matter how you wanna carry that shit," Jared growled.

"Nah, I'm just going to let her ass suffer. Yeah, we've done some stupid shit before, and both of us have cheated, but damn after this cancer thing, we were supposed to have been on some real *us* shit. Never would I have thought she'd let a nigga hit raw though, J," I expressed.

"Take it from the top, how did you find this shit out?"

After explaining everything to him, Jared sat there with a stunned ass face. It was the same face I made when I saw Tina lopsided, half cement, fake ass, bad weave wearing ass, helping her to the car. I just could not believe the shit, and I was watching it with my own fucking eyes.

"Real shit, I'm sorry this happened to you, little bro. I know you really love that friendly ass chick. But you knew what it was from jump! The day you came home with her, talking about she was your girl, I told you what it was. Granted, I gave you my blessing to move how you felt because you were love-struck, but I warned you about the time she was on.

Shorty always been a clout chaser. I told you to be careful with this dizzy ass bitch. She was always looking for the clout even back then. I told my niggas she was off-limits, but at some point, we all kinda saw this coming," Jared spoke his truth from the heart.

"You did. I should've listened, but she already had a hold on my heart," I replied.

All I could do was hang my head low because, as usual, my big brother called 'flaw' on the shit he saw in someone that I couldn't see.

"I'm done for real, bro," I sighed.

"Respect. Now, tell me what else is on your mind," he questioned, giving me the all-knowing side-eye.

Chuckling, I wrinkled my nose at the same time he did. Damn, our mannerisms were almost identical, even though our personalities were opposites. I knew I needed to talk all of this out, and I would've told him before anyone else anyway. So, I gave him the rundown of the news that Chantel and her co-worker, Pamela told me earlier.

"You a whole damn liar! Put it on granddaddy grave. You lying!" he swore.

"I swear on granddaddy grave. I might be a dad in 9 months if this mystery lady's body accepts my sperm. I always thought all my kids would be by Alana, but clearly, that shit didn't go as planned and maybe for a good reason," I spoke humbly.

"When do we meet ya baby mom's?" he queried.

"Chantel and I are going to her job tomorrow to see what we can work out. You know I'm not living without my seed in my life, so something will have to give," I strongly stated.

"I can come with you for support, back-up, muscle whatever you need. I haven't seen my bae in a while anyway. You sure you don't need me?" he asked, flexing his triceps.

"Chantel ain't thinking about you. And nah, we should be good, but if I need you, I know how to reach you. I'm staying here tonight; I'm exhausted from this draining ass day. I'm going to bed after I shower. The maid did clean-up my sheets from the last time I stayed, right? Is my bed already turned down for the night?" I asked half-jokingly.

"You don't have a room here. I keep telling you that shit. And you know she changes the sheets whenever you stay. She better, that is what she gets paid for. Take your spoiled ass to bed," he laughed, dismissing me with his hands making the peasant fingers gesture.

"Hey! Real shit, I'm going to marry that girl," Jared called out to my back as I walked towards the bedroom.

The sun peeked through the crack in the curtains, causing me to stir in my slumber. I groaned at the sound of the birds chirping loudly. What the hell were they so happy about this early in the morning? The sheets were tangled around my body from the tossing and turning I did all night. Using the palm of my hand to rub the sleep out of eyes, I stumbled to the window to shut the curtains completely. In a huff, I fell back to the bed, kicking my boxers off, allowing me to get completely comfortable before allowing the sandman to take over my body again.

"Noah, Chantel's here waiting on you in the living room. She said she called you numerous times but didn't get an answer, so she came over. She probably really came through to lay eyes on me but get up so y'all can go see about my niece or nephew," Jared spoke, standing at the edge of the bed.

"What time is it?" I croaked, my throat dry as hell.

"It's almost 9 a.m.," he replied easily.

"Shit, let me get up and dressed for the day."

"Okay, take your time. I'm going to go get breakfast for Chan. Maybe make wedding plans and shit," he chuckled.

My eyes rolled up to the ceiling, all I could do was chuckle with him. Jared left me alone to get ready. When I got out of the shower, my stomach growled at the smell of bacon. I wondered if Jared made breakfast himself or if he called his chef over. I knew that the chef normally only worked on the weekends. Lance was the best cook I've ever had the pleasure of tasting. I mean, I'd never say that around my mother, but the man could burn. Jared's busy schedule meant he wasn't home often during the week. Most of his free time came on the weekends.

You'd think he had a real 9 to 5, but my brother was one of the biggest drug dealers on the East Coast. I could have followed in his footsteps, but instead, I went to NC State University to obtain a degree in Engineering. I had a full ride, but Jared and my parents made sure I had everything I needed. My parents sent me money for the basics, but Jared kept me fly as hell. He was so proud when I walked across that stage. Now, I owned a top engineering firm that I built from the ground up. Not one to be stuffed in my office all day, I could normally be found at the construction site with my hard hat and Timb's on. But at any given moment, I could switch back to the tailored suits and red bottoms for the board meetings.

Emerging from the bedroom fully dressed and ready to head out, I found Chantel perched on the counter with Jared standing between her legs, feeding her fruit from his plate. These two should just call it what it is and be together again. A few years back, they dated, but when Chantel told Jared she refused to have sex with anyone again until marriage, he walked. Her heart was broke, but it was the right decision for her at the time. She had been in and out of relationships with losers. Jared was so used to pussy being thrown to him from every direction, he was not willing to live with her restrictions. However, he loved her too much to cheat on her like he'd do anyone else.

"Am I interrupting something?" I asked coyly.

Chantel tried to jump off the counter like she was caught making out for the first time by her parents. Jared wrapped his arms around her, not letting her move past him. After whispering God knows what in her ear, he began to kiss her lips. Her cheeks looked like they were burning hot, she blushed so hard. Chantel squeezed her eyes shut tightly, sucking her lips inside her mouth to stop the widespread grin that threatened to cross her face.

"No, I'm ready," she said.

Jared snuck another kiss, helping her to the ground. My phone rang. Once I saw it was my office, I left them in the kitchen, heading to the living room. After taking care of some business that couldn't wait, I doubled back to the kitchen to find Jared gone and Chantel putting the dishes away.

"Y'all didn't leave me anything to eat?" I scoffed.

"Of course, it's in the microwave. Warm it up and let's go; you can eat it in the car," she demanded, rushing me.

Chapter Three

GIANNA

From Bad to Worse

"Good morning, Dana," I greeted my niece by marriage.

"Hey, Auntie," she cheerfully responded, hobbling out of the driver's side of her Kia Soul.

I reached the back door of my bakery before her. As usual, she was moving slow as hell. Dana was only 21, but she weighed over 300 pounds, so everything she did seemed to be in slow motion. The logic of her working all day in a bakery shop just didn't make sense, causing the pounds to pile on even more. I hated to see her slowly killing herself this way, but every time I expressed my concerns to my husband and his family, they told me it was her life to destroy.

"I can't wait to eat this food, I'm starving!" she spoke as soon as she passed me at the door.

"Well, while I look over the calendar for today, go ahead and take a seat in the front," I offered.

On the inside, I was fuming because I like to come to my shop ready to work every day. Family or not, if I'm ready, all my employees should be ready. Instead of pointing out that fact to her, I wanted her to get as far as possible away from me while she ate her breakfast. I swear she didn't chew but just made weird sucking noises as she inhaled the food down her throat. Licking her chapped lips, she smiled at the bag that held the fast-food breakfast she had in her hand. I cringed, turning my back to her. I went to wash my hands so I could get started.

My eyes quickly scanned the special orders I had lined up for today, mentally putting in order what I needed to start first. Choosing the tea and specialty coffee of the day, each delicious aroma began to penetrate the air. Promptly at 9 a.m. every morning, Two Sweets opened its doors. When I opened the doors of my shop for the very first time, it was a feeling I still couldn't describe with words. The pride that flowed within my veins that day was a feeling I never wanted to forget. My mother taught me how to bake from an incredibly young age, and it had always been my passion. Even without peeking to the front, I knew that my regulars would be outside waiting for me to open as early as 15 minutes before opening time. The love I was shown on a daily basis from my customers made my heart glow.

On the menu for this morning was mango coconut muffins, cinnamon rolls, and strawberry scones. After getting each pastry in the oven, I started to take out what I needed to prep for the special orders that were being picked up today. Upon hearing the back door open, I peeked around the corner, greeting my employee Toni as she entered the bakery.

"Hey, Mrs. Wesley. Good morning!" she greeted chipperly with a wide smile.

Returning the smile and energy, I asked her how she was doing this morning. After exchanging small talk for a few minutes, she walked off to wash her hands and put on her apron. I heard her speak to Dana as she politely asked her to flip the chairs down off the table and wipe them down for the people that would be dining in this morning. Dana's lazy ass grunted her response. She didn't want to take orders from Toni, but she didn't have a choice. If Dana wasn't my husband's only niece, I would have been fired her. It's nothing more I hate than a lazy person with no ambition. She had so much life to live in front of her, but she was content with working part-time for me just to say she had a job.

While my hands were full of the ingredients, my phone rang, and my neck craned to see who was calling me. My eyes rolled involuntarily once I saw it was my husband- Mayor William Wesley. My phone read as it rang back to back. I wondered what the fuck he wanted, knowing that this time of the morning was always my busiest. It was just like him to be inconsiderate and mess up my flow. Finally, tired of the back to back calls, I dropped everything on the counter I used for my workspace and snatched up the phone.

"Yes, William?" I answered the phone, hostilely.

"Well damn, good morning to you too, wife. Did you miss me and wake up on the wrong side of the bed?" he joked.

"If that's what you want to call it," I replied dryly.

"I know your busy, baby, but I just wanted to tell you to have a great day. I'll be home tonight, I got you a gift," he boasted.

"I didn't need a gift but thank you. Have a safe trip home," I added gingerly.

"You okay, baby?" William questioned.

I cringed at the sound of him calling me, baby. William was such a selfish asshole. He didn't love me, he just needed me to keep his image pure. At one point, I thought we were both head over heels for each other, but the joke was on me. Just like right now, he thought I believed him about having to meet with a couple of mayors and senators out of state for a week. Two days after he left, his secretary called me looking for him. I guess his dumb ass forgot to clue his office in. He told his people at work my father was having serious surgery, and he needed to be there to support his family. When she couldn't reach him after two days of trying, she reached out to me.

"I'm great actually, just prepping for my busy day. You know the store is about to open," I sighed, tired of the pleasantries.

"I didn't even check the time, just wanted to hear your voice, baby. Love you," he breathed in the phone.

"Love you too. Safe travels. I gotta go, baby," I stressed.

Once I hung up the phone, I gagged at having to call him

baby and pretend everything was peachy. However, I refused to let on that I was on to his bullshit before I had everything set up to move out and on. Focused on the task in front of me, I spoke as Trey floated in the building to begin his shift as the cashier. Quickly, I glanced at the clock on the wall to check the time. Chuckling, he said he was not only on time but had five minutes to spare. All I could do was giggle and shake my head. Trey was always floating in at the last minute, but he was almost never late.

"Good ahead and open the doors," I hollered to the front.

"Yes, ma'am," Trey answered.

Even from the back of the kitchen, I could hear the rush of the bakery. I smiled inwardly. I knew the rush would be constant for about two hours straight. Which is why I had been slowly adding on more employees. While only being open for six months, my name was slowly becoming a household name in my town. I was beyond flattered.

"OH HELL NO!" I heard a man's voice shout.

My ears perked up instantly, so I could hear what was happening out there. Briskly, I washed my hands, heading out to the front to find out what was going on. We never had any problems or chaos in the store, so my heart was beating rapidly.

"Chantel, this chick cannot be my baby momma, man! You let your office accidentally give my sperm to her? My baby gone be ugly! I can't have an ugly baby! I mean, I'll love the baby, and we will just have to dress it fly as fuck but aughh...damn, man. How I'm supposed to show baby pictures to all my friends and my jit will be looking like a baby wilde-beest?" the dude yelled.

I froze. Wait, if he asked for a Ms. Wesley, Dana would've answered since we shared the same last name. He said his sperm, I automatically knew he was there for me. Right at that moment, I made up my mind to sue the company for breaching my privacy. There is no way he should know who I am, let alone where I work. Not sure how to handle this, I plastered a mean sneer on my face as I rounded the corner.

"Do we have a problem out here? Can I help you?" I spat.

Slowly, the gentleman lifted his head off of his companion's shoulders to face me. My breath hitched in my throat. This man was fine as hell; my body betrayed me. My heart began pounding, my attitude was gone in an instant as I thought about how beautiful our baby would be. If he was who I thought he was, I'm wasn't sure of how the mix up happened. Nervously, I used both hands to smooth down my apron. Everyone was just standing there in shock, not sure what to say.

Trey loudly whispered, "Dana, you didn't tell us you were looking for a sperm donor."

"I didn't, this man is delusional," she scoffed.

"Sir, how can I assist you today? I don't appreciate this rude disruption in my store," I remarked.

"Sorry, I didn't come here to cause a scene," he apologized.

When he spoke in a tone that I presumed to be his regular voice, my thighs clenched. His voice vibrated through my body, sounding like hot sex on a platter. It had been almost a year since I had sex with my husband William, which made it even easier to make up my mind to move on. The biggest factor was the fact that he refused to have kids with me, even though it was something we had always discussed prior to marriage and during the first years that we had gotten married. Now, he barely looked at me, and sex was out of the question. Before it just stopped, he began to demand that we use condoms, but we had never used condoms previously. It pissed me off that he thought I would try to trap his ass when I would never do that to him or anyone else.

Offering them a seat at one of the tables, I sat down with them, asking again how I could help them or what the problem was. His gaze had me squirming in my seat. It was like he was taking my clothes off inch by inch, in his head. It felt as if it was just the two of us at the table until the pretty lady he was with cleared her throat, bringing us out of the trance we were stuck in. My eyes looked up to meet hers, I take back the word pretty. She was beautiful, her skin the color of baked cinnamon. She had jet black hair, that flowed softly around her heart shaped face in a bob. The lady had a perfect button-shaped nose, slanted, black tinted eyes, high cheekbones, and her lips held a flawless pout that was covered in a nude tinted lipstick.

"Again, I'm sorry for causing a scene. Long embarrassing story short, I had testicular cancer, and to make sure I'd be able to be a father and have my own family, I had my sperm frozen. I found out that my sperm was given to Ms. Wesley by accident, and I just lost it. I didn't mean any disrespect, but my sperm wasn't meant for her," he sighed.

"I'm the Mrs. Wesley that used your sperm, not my husband's niece," I stuttered.

"Wait, what?" he stammered.

"I can't talk about this right now, but can you come back after I close the shop, please? We close at 4 p.m. today, I'm not sure why the agency hasn't called me. I am so sorry this happened to you two. I can't even imagine how you must be feeling," I offered sincerely.

"I'm his sister," the lady spoke up.

"Please don't call the agency until after I meet you back here tonight. Even though my sister didn't make the mistake, she works at the clinic where the switch took place. I just want to protect as many people as possible. If that's okay," he rasped.

"Can you be back at 6 p.m.?"

"Only if you let me have a mango-coconut muffin on the house," he teased with a glimmer in his eye.

I agreed. My mind was racing, I couldn't help but think that this man as my baby daddy was going to cause an uproar in my life that I wasn't ready for. After getting a confirmation that they'd be back later in the evening, I offered my first name, also asking for theirs. Not wanting to leave Chantel out, I offered for her to come with me to pick out what she wanted. When I walked them to the door, we said goodbye's promising to meet later this evening. As soon as I turned around, my staff was over talking each other, trying to get the scoop on what just happened. I bounced from one leg to the other, telling them that I handled everything, but I needed to get back to baking because the first pick-ups were in less than two hours. After shutting down any other questions, I returned to the kitchen, slipping my headphones in my ears to drown out my thoughts so I could focus on getting my orders out.

Chapter Four

ALANA

Mad At The World

"The number you have reached," the automated system sang in my ear.

Infuriated that Rico changed his number on me after the fuck shit he pulled yesterday, I flung my phone across the room, causing it to crash into the wall. I screamed as the phone fell apart in pieces, and it popped against the brick into the floor. The audacity of this nigga! Did he forget who the fuck he was dealing with? I'll ride through the West Side and shut all that shit down, with his clown ass.

Before Chantel left the house to meet with Noah, she dropped some heavy shit on me. The news of him possibly having a baby on the way with a chick none of us has ever met, let alone heard of, fucked up my mental. I knew it was an accident, but it sure felt like I was hit with instant karma from the foul shit I pulled by getting pregnant. I just couldn't wrap my head around it; I was the only woman alive that was supposed to bear his kids. Whoever this chick was must have been desperate to get sperm from the sperm bank unless her situation was something like ours. Either way, she better be prepared for us to be in this baby's life and co-parent.

Gulping the pills from the clinic down my throat, I chased half a bottle of water behind it. Frustrated didn't even begin to put into words how I felt. Rico's bitch ass lied to me about using protection, he thought that shit was cute when it wasn't. The dick was feeling so good in the moment, I didn't double-check to make sure he had strapped up when he flipped my ass over and dove deep in my guts. I don't know what kinda voodoo Rico had in his stroke, but it had the power to make a bitch smack her momma. Even as I sat on the edge of the bed with a broken phone, shattered ego, and my insides sucked out, I reminisced about that death stroke he delivered. Expertly.

I cracked my knuckles, easing some of the tension in my body. I didn't know what to do next. Should I confront Rico first for treating me like a random slut bucket? Or Noah for not calling me this morning to talk this shit out? Yes, I fucked up majorly, but Noah and I were for life! Nothing or no one would ever come between us. It'd take a while, but we'd get past this like we got past everything else. I loved Noah with all my heart, but this pussy of mine be needing some shit he just hasn't been able to provide lately. Not that I'd leave him in his time of need, but this thing between my legs has a mind of her own. Noah would still suck the soul out my body, but after a while, it just wasn't enough. I decided to take a shower to get my day started. I had moves to make starting with running up on Rico's dumb ass.

My body glistened from my Kaylux Vacation Body Highlighter, the soft glimmer was perfect for my unmatched beauty. My beauty radiated from my pores. I knew I should be humble about how pretty I was, but why should I be? God didn't create us all equal. It wasn't my fault he took his time to make me this perfect. Deep, nutmeg-hued skin, natural long jet-black hair down to my waist, my eyes were the color of warm Hennessey, my ass fat, it wasn't nothing on me that said I wasn't worth a nigga's whole check. Everywhere I went, I turned heads, male and female. My sister and I looked so much alike, but I was taller than her by an inch or two. She was always timid in ways that I wasn't. Whereas I always went for exactly what I wanted.

When I reached for my iPhone, I grew aggravated with Rico again for pissing me off to the point that I destroyed my damn phone. Inhaling sharply, I crouched down in front of the decorative brick wall picking up the pieces to the phone. After I threw the broken pieces in the trash, I threw on a hot pink sundress with some clear soled wedges. It was time to make my appearance on the West Side, Rico would have to answer to me today! I decided to stop by my girl Tina's so she could roll with me to the mall to get a new phone and to have her with me when I ran up on Rico's bitch ass.

My face scrunched up whenever I pulled up to Tina's hood. I wished she'd follow my lead and step to some ballers that had pockets deep enough to change her life. Her ass was still living in the projects with her mother, sister, nephew, and older brother. A whole household of nobodies. If she wasn't my best friend from elementary school, I would've been left her ass on the hood level. Tina has had my back since 2nd grade, so we were loyal to each other. Honestly, she was my only ugly friend because I refused to be seen this a bunch of muggly looking hoes. My crew was the shit, and we knew it.

Banging on the heavy steel door, I waited for someone to yell for me to come in. Most of the time the whole house was home sitting around being deadbeats. That shit made my skin crawl, I couldn't take being around people with no ambition. I didn't have to work more than a part-time job myself because my man made sure I was a kept woman.

"It's open," Tina's brother shouted.

"Hey, everyone," I greeted, walking through the front door.

The smell of candles burning caught my nose. I wasn't able to make out the scent, but it filled the whole house. One thing I could say was, even though it was five people living in this little two-bedroom apartment, it was always clean and always smelled great.

"Hey," Tina's mom replied, while everyone else in the living room just hit me with a head nod.

Since I've been here a million times plus one, I excused myself out of the way of the tv, walking back to Tina's room. Without knocking on the door, I barged into her personal space, pouncing on her bed.

"Bitch, wake yo' ass up! I need to go get a new phone and run up in Rico's hood," I told her.

"I'm tired, hoe. You woke me up early yesterday, remember?" she uttered, yanking the cover over her head.

"So, you going to let your best friend go out here without back up?" I pouted, knowing playing the loyalty card would get her out the bed.

Tina rolled her eyes, slowly rising from the bed.

"I knew you loved me," I said excitedly.

"What happened to your phone?"

"Rico changed his number, and it pissed me off, so I threw it against the decorative brick wall in my bedroom. I wasn't thinking straight."

"Dumb ass go get another phone while I get myself together. I need to take a bath and brush my teeth," she stated.

"Alright, bet. Thanks, bestie," I exclaimed.

She didn't even respond; she just walked out the room towards the bathroom in the hallway. Still sitting on the bed, I watched her until she shut the bathroom door. I shook my head silently in disgust, my girl needed to get her lopsided ass fixed. Always the thirsty one, she went to an underground filling party and fucked her body up. I told her not to go to that bullshit plumping party. If she would've just followed my lead, she would have been able to finesse some dude out the money to get the work done properly on her body. But she likes instant gratification, instead of thinking shit through. Happy that she went along with my plan for the day, I skipped out the house to go get another phone.

Once I had my phone in my hand, my first call was to Tina letting her know that I was on my way back to get her. She confirmed she was ready to go, saying she pulled out her brass knuckles in case anyone wanted to pop fly. Tina was a wild one, and I loved every minute of it. I hoped it wouldn't come to that because, honestly, my stomach was starting to cramp. However, I knew Rico wasn't expecting me to show up the very next day and wreck shop, but I was on my way. It was time to show him the hood never left me. I left it.

Chapter Five

CHANTEL

Twilight Zone

"Yes," I huffed into the phone.

"Stop with that fake shit, bae," Jared growled into the phone.

I fastened my seatbelt, waiting a bit before responding, giving my Bluetooth time to pick up.

"Bae?" he questioned.

"The car was picking you up, I just saw you this morning. Don't think this is about to be something it's not J-Black," I taunted, knowing he hated when I call him by his street name.

"I see you on that bs today. Don't call me that shit. It ain't for you and doesn't belong on your lips. But since you think you know that side of me, ride out with me today. I need a pretty young thing on my arm."

"Ride out with you where? And does this include lunch? If not, I have things to do."

"We can go to lunch, or you can be lunch," he smoothly said.

"Ain't this why we broke up? Because you couldn't taste it?"

"You're about to be my wife soon, I can wait. But I'll feed your greedy ass, where are you? Did y'all meet my niece or nephew's momma?" he asked.

"Yes, she's stunning! Noah lost his mind when he thought it was this other chick that answered to the same last name at her bakery. She serves some good stuff in there too! I can't wait to go back. She asked us to come back after the store closes, and she has time to clean up," I advised.

"What time is that?"

"Noah said he was going alone. She's gorgeous, and he's freshly single, so I'm sure he's going to try to push up on her. The rest of my day is free," I offered.

"Say less, meet me at the house. You can park your car and ride with me."

"On my way," I stated, hanging up in his ear.

Flying down the highway blasting 90's R&B, I made it to his house in record time. I pulled into the driveway next to Jared's brand new shiny blue Porsche Panamera. Getting out of my car, I moved slowly walking around his car to get a good look at it. This car was everything. It wasn't anything about me that was flashy, but I could definitely see myself in this car.

"You ready?" Jared asked, startling me because I didn't hear him come out the house.

"Umm, yeah," I stammered.

"You good?"

"Yes, you scared me," I giggled.

"That's 'cause you were out here creeping around my car like you were trying to steal that bitch," he laughed.

"Shut up," I said, opening my car door after sliding on my shades to block the summer sun.

The instant we backed out the driveway, he casually floated his hand to my exposed thigh. I swallowed hard but managed to keep a straight face, this may not have been a good idea after all. We were headed on the opposite side of town, he told me that he needed to make a stop before lunch. Since it was still early in the day, I had no complaints. Reclining my seat back, I got comfortable. Jared glanced over at me with a smile that sent butterflies twirling in the pit of my stomach, turning up the music. He began to rap along with the song that now blasted through the speakers.

My eyes fluttered open as Jared tapped my inner thigh before gripping it tightly, I'm not sure how I managed to fall asleep with the bass booming in my ears.

"Hmm, we're here, bae."

"Can I just stay in the car?"

"Nah, I have someone I want you to meet. Nothing crazy though."

Silently, I glared at him before agreeing to get out the car. Snatching up some gum from the middle console, I popped a piece in my mouth, refusing to meet someone with my breath still half sleep. My eyes gazed around my surroundings, I realized we were on the West Side in the Liberty Own's projects. Since I grew up in the projects being here didn't bother me. My mother worked hard to get us out of that situation, even though it took years. Alana was seventeen when she moved out to be with her boyfriend. My mother tried to stop her, but Alana wasn't hearing shit she had to say.

At the time, I was only 13 and didn't want to be alone while my mother worked two jobs to not only support us but to save for our new home. However, nothing we said made Alana stay home. My mother grew exhausted from dealing with the trouble Alana was causing her, so eventually, she gave up the fight. My mom said she wished she could save Alana from herself, but she was only 3 months away from being grown anyway. She begged her to stay home, finish school, pick a career, and to go to college. Alana refused, so my mother bowed to defeat.

*A*s soon as Jared's feet touched the pavement, every bitch in the complex was calling his name like he was some type of ghetto celebrity. On the inside I was steaming, did he bring me out here to see that everyone wanted him so I could be jealous? But then the dudes started to swarm us, and I realized he seriously was just the man everyone wanted to show love to. Introducing me as his wife, the men looked jealous that I wasn't on their arm, and the women began to roll their eyes. I heard someone suck their teeth.

One bitch jumped slick saying that she didn't see a ring on my finger. He shut her ass down so quick I had to chuckle. It was then I took his hand in mine, whispering in his ear to ask him who it was he wanted me to meet.

"Aww shit. Rico, here come your wild ass baby mom's yo'," I heard someone shout over the crowd.

The very next voice I heard was Alana's. My eyes searched the crowd trying to get a view on my sister and this Rico dude. Jared shifted his attention to Rico with a look that could murder. Rico threw up his hands, timidly walking backward as if to say he didn't want any smoke. It was too late, the crowd all gasped at once as I heard glass shattering nearby. Alana's crazy ass was holding a bat, breaking every window out of a dubbed out gray, old school Supreme Cutlass. Rico starting cussing, running towards my sister. Jared shouted to him that he better not lay a fucking finger on her, which made Rico pause in mid-run. Slowly, he turned around speaking in Spanish to Jared. The crowd parted quietly as Jared slowly strolled to Rico and Alana. Still holding his hand, I walked right behind him, ignoring the groans of the women around us.

"J-Black, she came out here on some bullshit, man! You know that car is my baby, why you are protecting this bitch?" Rico complained.

"I know damn well you knew that was my sister when you went up in her raw. I already told everybody out here to ignore her ass if she came out this way. Don't try the innocent shit with me, Rico," Jared spat, his eye jumping with anger.

"Tell him who I am, Black! Let him know he played the wrong bitch!" Alana shouted as she smashed the hood with the bat she was still holding.

"Alana, take your wild ass home. I won't allow him to fuck you up. He should, hell I should. You out here acting all fucking dumb over some dick that you shouldn't even fucking have had a thought bubble about," Jared sneered between his clenched teeth.

"Tina, you should've stopped your girl from coming out here making stupid ass decisions. Instead, you out here egging her dumb ass on. Both of you need to grow the fuck up!" Jared snorted, reading them both.

"Fuck you, Jared, J-Black, whatever or whoever you want to be today! You weren't calling me dumb when I was sucking your dick. Let's talk about that shit," Alana hollered.

Her words knocked the wind out of my lungs. Did my sister just say she used to suck my man's dick? Well, ex-man, but damn, I was here with him.

"When you used to what, Lana?" I asked breathlessly.

"I said what I said. He just like the rest of these no-good ass niggas. Yeah, now he calls me sis, because he was with you and you're my sister but don't get that shit twisted his snake done slithered down my throat too many times to count," she admitted vulgarly.

Scanning Jared's face, I searched for the truth. Much to my surprise, he didn't have a comeback, and my heart crumbled in front of all the people surrounding us. I let out a scorned cackle, pushing Jared out the way as he stood there dumbfounded by the way she let the cat out the bag. I balled up my fist, throwing a haymaker right to her face, knocking her ass out on the spot. Violently, I spun around, punching Jared square across the jaw. As he reached up to grab his face, I plucked the keys out of his hand, marching rapidly through the crowd to his car. He was calling my name behind me, telling me to wait so he could explain. Fuck him and her scum bucket ass. I was done with both of those dirty muthafuckas. After I adjusted the seat in his car, I pulled off as he started banging on the window. I didn't even feel bad about taking his car and leaving him. Hell, he the man in this hood, right? His snake slithering ass will figure out how to get home. As I turned the corner, I called Noah with tears in my eyes.

"Bestie, you ain't going to believe this shit," I sniffled.

Chapter Six

NOAH

The Cat's Out The Bag

Frozen, I listened to my best friend rant, cry and cuss about Alana giving Jared head. Stuck between telling her the truth or lying to her about already knowing, I stayed silent while she got everything out of her system. Once she paused to take a breath, I spoke up.

"I knew," I whispered lowly.

"What? What you mean you knew?" she barked hatefully.

"This was before she and I got together. When I first brought her over to the house, Jared told me to leave her alone because she was for everybody. I confronted her, and she told the truth about it. She said she wasn't on that type of time anymore. She promised since we had been together, she had chilled. We all came to an agreement to put the past behind us. When you started dating Jared, we all collectively decided to keep it buried. It was not important anymore.

Jared wanted to tell you, I said you'd never date him if you knew. She was giving all the boys head, back in high school. Don't act like you don't remember, she got suspended three times over it. You weren't even in high school, yet. I didn't want him to lose out on the special person you are because your sister is a hoe. I'm sorry if you feel deceived," I apologized.

The weight of the secret evaporated in the thin air, instantly making me feel better. I had been carrying that around on my conscience for a few years now. It was the only secret I've held from Chantel, in all these years.

Silence filled the phone line. When she started talking again, I could hear the torment in her voice.

"You knew and loved her anyway?" she croaked out.

"Yes," I replied softly.

"Why would she embarrass me in front of all of those people? I'm convinced she was referring to something more recent. At this point, I cannot put it past her or him for that matter."

"Chan, I can guarantee you Jared would never betray me or you that way for it to be even remotely recent. Even back then, he went around making sure no dudes would deal with her because I was her man. He said just to make him feel better about us being together and having my heart on the line. Plus, despite what you think because of the break-up y'all had, Jared is in love with you. He has been for a very long time," I honestly spoke.

"Jared loves Jared. But I can agree that he loves you almost as much as he loves himself. I'm pissed that you kept this from me, but I also understand in a way. I just wish I never dealt with him in that way. At least I was never intimate with him after he was doing it with my sister," she breathed into the phone.

"They have never had sex, ever. And yes, he left you when you declined to sleep with him because he knew he was not stronger than his flesh at the time. He even sat down and talked to my parents about it, told them he loved you but also needed to have sex. Our father said if he could not make the sacrifice of waiting, to let you go. My mother agreed, telling him it would hurt more if he cheated on you, and you found out. She said to let you go, but someone else may see how special you are, and he may not ever get you back," I informed her.

Hearing soft sobs on the other end of the phone, alerted me to the fact that she still loved Jared as much he loved her. I wished they'd work out their differences because truth be told they were amazing together. Just thinking back, I've never seen Jared so in sync with any female. Alana and I had been together since 11th grade. However, the chemistry we shared was not as strong or noticeable as Jared and Chantel's.

"Chan, don't cry. We both know when Alana is hurt, she lashes out to hurt everyone around her. She's toxic. Nothing more, nothing less. Hey, those muffins were great but wearing off. Come scoop me so we can go to lunch, that way you can tell me what to ask Gianna."

After lunch with Chantel, I had her swing by my condo to get some personal things to take back to Jared's for a few nights. The plan was not to stay with him forever. This morning I made up my mind to buy my own house. It was time, especially if I have a baby coming into the world. I needed to make sure my life was stable as possible. I'd allow Alana to keep the condo, transferring everything in her name. Never would I want to see her out on the street. She'd live on the street before crawling home to her mother to admit failure.

Chantel drove me back to Jared's, where she left his car in the driveway, exchanging it out for her car. Promising to call her as soon as I finished meeting with Gianna, I sprinted in the house to use the restroom. My thoughts circled my head. So much had happened in the last 24 hours. I decided to take a nap to clear my mind, so I could focus on Gianna once I got back to the bakery this evening.

Fresh out of the shower, I double checked my appearance in the mirror. Even though we'd already met for the first time this morning, I wanted to give off a good impression. I prayed she was at least a pretty lady, but Gianna was more than that, she was breathtaking. I had the first day of school jitters. Moisturizing my beard, I grabbed some Carmex to make sure my lips weren't crusty. I cracked my neck to relieve some tension, forcing my shoulders down to take the stress off them.

Suddenly at a loss for words, Gianna unlocked the door for

me. I gawked with my eyes damn near popping out of the sockets, taking her in. She looked so different from this morning. She was already gorgeous, but earlier she had on an oversized apron, a hairnet, and some clogs.

Her radiated under the soft glow of the bakery lights above us.

"Hey, welcome back," she grinned, offering me her hand to shake.

"Damn," I muttered.

"Is something wrong?" she asked with her brows knitted together.

"I'm sorry, you are just stunning. I'm in amazement at how beautiful you are," I spoke truthfully.

Her mouth drew up in a slow smile, easily showing off her all her perfect pearly whites.

"Flattery will get you nowhere. But come in so we can talk," she giggled.

"It's not flattery when it's the truth," I countered, winking at her.

"Okay, surprise baby momma, tell me about yourself," I inquired after I got situated in my seat.

"Well, I'm married, but my husband didn't want kids out of the blue after it had been our dream to start a family for years. I just found out his reason; he has been cheating. I guess it isn't a need to start a family with someone you don't plan on being with for the long term.

I'm 26, my birthday is next week, so I'll be 27 on the 27th.

Which makes me a Cancer, I didn't want to wait anymore. My father is a prominent minister in this area, my mother a homemaker; she is the one who taught me to bake. Hence, why I'm the proud owner of this bakery, which has always been my dream. I am an only child, but I'm close to the cousins on my mother's side of the family. I believe in the Holy Trinity. Religion is very important to me. It's the center of my life, God is the center of my life. Whewww, okay your turn," she rasped.

"Happy early birthday, I need to put that in my calendar to make sure I get you a good baby momma gift," I chuckled.

"You don't have to do that. We don't even know if it took anyway!" she exclaimed.

"Well, if it didn't, we'll try again," I said, shrugging my shoulders easily.

"Wow, just like that? You were outraged this morning. With good reason to be, I must add."

"Aye, shit happens. You want this baby and so do I. As long as we can come to some type of agreement, I believe we can make it work."

"Tell me more about yourself, please," she pleaded, shifting her eyes to her lap.

"I'm an Aries, younger than you just by a little bit. My birthday is on April 11th, so I just turned 26. As I informed you earlier, I was diagnosed with cancer early, but thank God I caught it in time. I own my own construction company. I have a degree in Engineering, my parents are still together like yours. I have one older brother, who I still look up to. He can't wait to meet you by the way. I came from a loving family, but I haven't told my parents about the mix up yet.

My sister that was here with me this morning is actually my girlfriend's sister and my best friend. Well, my ex-girlfriend. Yesterday, I found out that she cheated and got pregnant by someone else. It tore me apart, then this bomb was dropped in my lap. But sitting here with you seems to cause the pain to melt away. I believe in God and fate," I concluded, reaching for her hand across the table.

We spoke for another hour getting to know each other's likes and dislikes. It was refreshing to meet someone like her that wasn't all labels and status. Getting to know each other a little more, we exchanged numbers. I told her I'd check in with her every day to make sure she was good. She promised that she would text me the appointment information for the end of next week when she found out if it took. She seemed relieved that I wanted to go along, and she didn't have to go through everything alone. Gianna confessed that it would probably take her parents some time to accept her decision, which is why she kept it to herself. She was afraid they'd try to talk her out of it, making or expecting her to stay with her husband no matter what.

It was no way in hell I'd let her go through this pregnancy alone. My father raised us to be upstanding, strong black men, and any child I were to bring into this world deserved the same thing.

I walked her out the back door, making sure she got to the

car safely, already feeling protective over the beautiful woman in front of me that could possibly be carrying my child. Declining her offer to drive me back around to the front of the store, I took my time walking back to my car, enjoying the evening air.

Chapter Seven

WILLIAM WESLEY

Honey, I'm Home

"I'll see you tomorrow at work, Sydney," I said, sliding out of the backseat of the car.

"Good night, Willie." She smiled softly.

After the driver handed me my bags from the trunk, I stood at the curb watching the black sedan pull away. It felt good to be back home. Even though I just came back from a week away with my mistress, I missed my wife. I needed to be back in her arms.

My mistress and I were away trying out a new treatment for HIV in another country. Sydney had heard about a guy in Costa Rica that was supposed to be studying under Dr. Sebi before he died. We decided to go check him out, what's the worst that could happen?

I couldn't bring myself to tell my wife that I had caught

HIV from a high scale sex party last year. Which is the only reason why I refused to have sex with her for almost a year. At first, I was in denial but decided to at least have protected sex with her. Once she started talking about starting the family we always dreamed of, I had a way out. I flipped everything on her, making her believe I didn't want any kids, even though I was longing for a family of my own. I made it seem that I refused to have sex with her because she'd try to trick me into getting her pregnant. It was the farthest thing from the truth. I was trying to save her life.

Glancing at the clock, I noticed it was after 5 p.m. which meant Gianna should be almost done in the bakery and would be home soon. Part of me wanted to go surprise her with dinner, but instead, I jumped in the shower to wash the long trip off me. I was emotionally exhausted. I wasn't sure how I'd be able to get back to Dr. Vargas without Gianna raising a fuss. We were due to go back next month and monthly for the next 8 months straight. He gave us all the tools to survive and live properly while being away from him, the problem was how the hell would I pull this off getting back and forth each month. If I didn't have a few millionaire drug dealers in my back pocket, I'd never be able to afford the luxury of going and living high off the hog while we were there.

Three months into my role as the mayor of my city, I made a deal with the biggest drug dealers to move the drugs out of the urban city areas. Instead of using their money, I had rehabs built. We made a deal that they could serve their fiends, in other areas and I wouldn't come after them. Proving how serious I was, the drug crews that were covering the areas I offered the guys I met with, I had arrested. They were all serving time from the corner boy to the boss. None of them were on the same level that the five guys I made the offer to. Each of them also had to give me one hundred thousand a year to stay in the game. Yes, it was dirty as hell, but I needed to figure out a treatment for me and my mistress. Still, every day, no matter the undercover things I did, I always put my city first. I just got myself caught up in some wild shit that goes on behind the doors of politics and rich people. I was doing everything in my power to fix what was broken around me, starting with my marriage.

The steam of our multi-jet shower system had the bathroom fogged up. Wiping the mirror to get a good look at myself, I smiled. I took a good look at myself, the bags under my eyes that were there the week before were gone. A slow smile spread across my face, maybe this was the beginning of my fresh start. My light grey eyes shimmered under the fluorescent light that hung over the bathroom vanity. I rubbed my hands through my naturally curly hair, taking note that I needed to schedule a haircut for later this week. My skin was beet red from the hotness of the water in the shower, my tortilla-colored skin tone made it easy for me to turn red under numerous different situations from a hot shower to being embarrassed.

Finally, finished with my hygiene practices in the bathroom, I scampered across the cold marble floor. Jumping online to order Gianna's favorite meal, I then texted her to let her know dinner was taking care of. Quickly, I prepared my own dinner, which was drastically different from what Gianna would be having. In order to make sure this treatment works, I needed to follow the instructions exceptionally close. It was no room for error or mistakes.

My bare feet heavily trudged around the kitchen, cleaning up the mess I made. Hastily, I jogged to the bedroom to grab my phone as I heard the alerts going off. Naturally, I assumed it was Gianna texting me back. However, when I checked the messages, it was all work-related. Growing irritated that she had not responded at all to my messages, I grabbed a shirt from the dresser, my mind made up to head out to the bakery.

Just as soon as I reached for the door handle, my phone went off in my hand. I saw it was Gianna, I relaxed some.

"Hey, baby. I was just about to come by the shop to check on you since you didn't respond," I told her.

"I'm just seeing your message. Thank you for dinner. I'll be home soon," she replied.

Gianna knew I was coming home today, and I reminded her this morning, so I'm not sure why she would work late. Sometimes the shit she does baffles me. She should have rushed home knowing I've been gone a full week. Her father was a well-respected, well-known Baptist pastor that raised her to follow her husband as the head of the household. I wasn't too pleased when she opened the bakery, but I understood she needed something to fill her days with since I often worked long hours. It's only been about six months that she's opened the shop, and business had been blooming. But it also seems she has a newfound confidence that I'm not completely sure I like.

Doordash rung the buzzer to let me know they were here, I buzzed them upstairs. The building security normally calls up to let the tenants know they have guests but the food deliveries they allow to ring up to the apartments themselves. Right after I paid the driver, Gianna stepped off the elevator rounding the corner, looking as good as ever.

Her long black hair bounced over her shoulder, the melanin in her skin popped against the bright yellow dress she wore. God must have dipped her in the silkiest, dark milk chocolate ever when he made her. Gianna's smile could light up the whole room, her lips were sensuously full, and she had the whitest set of teeth I've ever seen in my life. With the body of an African goddess, Gianna commanded any and every room she graced.

The pleasure was always the other person's when she entered a space. My wife was beautiful down to her toes. From her face to her ample bust, and a flat stomach leading to wide hips and bountiful booty. I'd never seen a man not do a double-take, including the Door Dash driver that just passed her in the hallway. As beautiful as she was, she was humble with a nurturing spirit. My wife was everything a man could wish for.

My eyes drunk her in greedily as she approached the front

door, embracing her as soon as she was within reach. Kissing my cheek, she returned the hug.

"Hey, baby," I greeted her.

"Hey, Wesley. Welcome home," she whispered in my ear.

Instead of calling me by my first name, Gianna has always called me by my last name, which I've always found sexy. Everything about her is one of a kind.

"You hungry? Let me get this set up for you, while you go wash the day off you," I suggested.

Once she returned from cleaning herself up and changing into a pair of sweats and a t-shirt, she came to sit at the table with me.

"You aren't eating with me?" she questioned, her eyebrows raised in surprise.

I've always had a raging appetite, so I knew this change wouldn't go unnoticed.

"I cheated and ate without you." I grinned.

"Funny choice of words, husband." She beamed brightly.

Wondering what she was talking about, my face twisted in a dumbfounded expression.

"What you mean, Gia? What was a funny choice of words?" I asked.

"You said you cheated."

"I meant I ate without you, baby. That's all," I stammered, my heart starting to beat. She couldn't possibly have found out anything, I covered my tracks well. It's no way she'd be able to get any information on my whereabouts. Reminding myself that I covered all bases and that if she did think I cheated on her, she wouldn't be this relaxed, I calmed myself down.

"Elizabeth called me to check on us a couple of days ago. How was my father doing? Did his surgery go well?" she taunted.

Gianna sweetly wiped her mouth with the napkin in front of her, then folded her hands together in front of her on the table. If looks could kill, I'd be a dead man. While she was still smiling, it was nothing but pure hatred looming in her eyes. Because I wasn't expecting to get caught, I had no lie prepared for this moment.

"Gianna, it's not what you think, baby. I promise," my voice croaked out, the guilt welling up in the back of my throat.

"Tell me what it is then, Wesley baby," she hissed through her teeth.

Inwardly, I knew she was about to boil over in anger. Gianna rarely yelled or raised her voice when she was upset. She said it took too much of her energy.

"I needed a breather and a get-away. Work has been more than I'm used to, and I needed to regroup. I didn't want to be selfish by asking you to come knowing that you need to focus on the bakery you just opened, babe," I said.

The words that fell from my lips were so convincing that I almost believed my own lie. Damn, I'm good. I knew I had her where I wanted her. She always complained that I didn't support her vision. This was a surefire way out of the jam she placed me in. Mentally, I gave myself a high-five for that comeback.

"Why didn't you tell me?" she countered.

"After making such a big fuss about you being a stay at home wife, I didn't think I should bring up I needed to take a vacation knowing you'd think I was trying to sabotage your business," I lied, laying it on thick.

"Everything slick don't slide, Wesley," she concluded.

"What the fuck does that mean?"

"It means... I know you went on vacation with Sydney. It means I know you're not fucking me, which means you have to be sleeping with her, and God only knows who else. It means I'm done with this marriage. I've given all I am willing to give. It means that I've taken the liberty of starting the family I want on my own, by using a sperm bank. I'll know within the next week or so if the sperm reached my eggs. Most importantly...it means GOODBYE," she rasped.

"You did what?" I yelled, jumping up, knocking the chair back to the floor.

"Thank you for our last meal together. I hope whoever you choose treats you as well as I tried to," she huffed, getting up from the table.

What the fuck just happened? The sudden onset of tears that sprung to my eyes burned as I tried to beg Gianna to sit down and just talk to me. All the air left my lungs like I had been punched in the chest repeatedly. I refused to allow the love of my love just to up and leave me. Running to dive in front of the door so she would not be able to get past me, I tried to stop her.

"Gianna, wait! Baby, just wait!" I exclaimed.

For the second time in the whole time we've been together and the second time tonight, she cussed, "Wesley, get the fuck out my way before I kill your ass."

Heartbroken, I allowed her to pass, but on the inside, I vowed to get my lady back. No matter the cost.

Chapter Eight

JARED

Big Brother Ish

"**W**hat they say?" I asked, jumping up from my seat as soon as Noah and Gianna bent the corner of the doctor's office.

Both of them had a blank expression on their face, indicating she wasn't pregnant. An awkward silence filled the air. Neither of them uttered a word, just motioned for us to go outside to talk.

"Shit," I cursed under my breath.

Nodding my head towards Chantel, giving her a signal to follow us, I plodded out of the waiting room in front of them. Disappointment settled in my bones. The excitement of being an uncle had me smiling since Noah shared the news. Suddenly, I was hit with an overwhelming feeling of needing to start my own family and soon. Immediately even. Not once had the thought of being a father crossed my mind before. I thought only women felt their biological clock ticking. What the hell?

We all stepped into the smoldering heat outside of the doctor's office, everyone's face looking glum. Noah took long strides towards Gianna's car, pausing once he reached the back bumper. Turning his body to face us with one foot perched up behind him on her bumper, he grabbed her hand into his, bringing her close to him before rotating her around to face us as well. Still, no words were spoken, my heart began to pump wildly.

"Tell us something, please," I shouted, tired of waiting.

"Yes!" Chantel pleaded in a strained voice.

Gianna glanced behind her. After they shared a pointed look, Noah finally opened his mouth to speak.

"She is indeed pregnant! We are having a baby!" he exclaimed, lifting her in the air.

His words left me in a trance, I stood there unable to move for a few seconds that felt more like an eternity. Chantel squealed, dancing around the parking lot with tears in her eyes. Briefly, I watched the sincerity of her happiness for them before I focused my full attention on Gianna and Noah.

"Congratulations! Oh shit, you're going to be a daddy, little bro! Damn, I'm so excited for y'all. You couldn't have found a better family to pro-create within, Gianna. We are going to love this baby so much. Welcome to the family, sis," I said, hugging her tightly.

"Thank you, I've prayed for the day I would become a

mommy. The blessing of parenthood is so beautiful. Noah has been so positive through this experience after finding out that I had his sperm instead of the person that it was meant for, that I'm already overwhelmed by the loving spirit of this family," she replied humbly.

Chantel had pinned Noah against the car, rocking him back and forth in her embrace with tears running down her eyes. She was so genuinely happy for them; she couldn't fight back the tears that were flowing freely down her face. Whispering something into Noah's ear, she let him go, now giving Gianna all her undivided attention. Slowly, she wiped the tears from her face congratulating Gianna. She tapped Gianna's arm, smiling brightly, saying she would be there every step of the way. Gianna graciously thanked her, saying she may need it because her family was going to flip out once they found out what she has done. Chantel snatched her into a hug, giving her a sisterly hug that looked like it would never end both of them sobbing.

"Okay, okay, Chantel. Let her go already. It's hot as hell out here, we need to get moving. Gia, I can call you that, right?" I questioned.

"Yes," she sniffled, releasing her arms from around Chantel.

"Listen, I know you haven't told your parents yet, but since it's official, let's do it tonight at my house. I can have my chef whip up some culinary greatness and have a small party. That way your parents and ours can find out at the same time.

We can celebrate together as the new blended family we are," I suggested.

I saw the hesitation on Gia's face, she suddenly looked fearful. Lightly, Noah touched her arm, explaining that this offer was a great way to bring everyone together, breaking the ice all at once. Another unspoken moment passed between them, the glimmer of hopefulness in Noah's eye caught me by surprise. I made a mental note to ask Noah just how close they had gotten over the last week. Even with no words spoken verbally, it was easy to see that their eyes were holding a private conversation between them.

Deeply sighing, Gianna returned her gaze to me, asking softly, "What time should we be there?"

"How about 6 o'clock? I have a few moves to make this afternoon, so that would give me time to handle my business first."

"I'll get started on a list for the chef and go grab some champagne. Well, I'll get sparkling apple cider for you, baby mama," Chantel stated.

After we all said our goodbyes for the moment, we went our separate ways for the rest of the day excited about the celebration of the evening. Chantel rode with me to the appointment. Since Noah explained the truth about Alana and me, she had forgiven all of us. Of course, we all had to promise to not hold anything else from her. She did allow me to wallow in my pity and embarrassment for a few days. Blowing up her phone with messages and calls is an understatement of the begging I did. I knew I was wrong for keeping it from her.

"Want me to drop you off or you riding with me today?"

"The last time I rode with you, I had to leave your disrespectful ass in the hood. You sure you're ready to try that again so soon?"

My eyes were already low from the weed I was smoking. Cutting my eye at her talking her shit, I stroked my beard in silence.

"No response, Jared? Does that mean you're taking me home?"

"If the decision was mine, you'd never leave my side, shorty. That's my word," I chuckled. I knew she'd think I was gaming, but I meant that shit.

"Where are you going today, Jared?" she smirked.

"Same hood, different hood, your hood, my hood, I have to go to two of the clinics, and I have a meeting with the mayor at 3," I answered honestly, returning the smirk.

"I need to get the stuff setup for the party. Buttttttttt, I'll ride with you for a little bit. Let's pray we both make it back to the house together, today," she sang.

Finally dropping Chantel off back at my house to get started on the party, I made my way downtown to the mayor's office after changing into more business-like attire. Throughout the day, I went through each hood where I held my drugs. I've never been the one to hold all my eggs in one basket. I kept everything. Even though I made an agreement with the mayor to not circulate the drugs in our communities, I still kept my work there. In the beginning, I was not with the changes he was trying to make, but my smart side won. No need to go to jail and give up my freedom when there was an option to simply change the location of what I was serving. Plus, it felt good to not make money off my own people killing them slowly.

"Hello, I have a meeting with Mayor Wesley," I communicated to the lady at the front desk.

"May I have your name, please?" she asked without even looking up from whatever she was studying on her desk.

Clearing my throat, I caused her to look at me. I hated a rude ass person, some of these people in this building tried to make you feel less than. Every time I stepped foot in this building, I had to demand my respect, respectfully. Truthfully, I was growing sick of meeting him here. This old bird in front of me was going to get cussed out soon, I felt it coming.

"My name is Jared Roberts," I declared after I had her full attention.

"Thank you, Mr. Roberts. I'll let him know that you're here," she spoke through clenched teeth.

Not giving her a response, I made my way back to the lobby to wait for someone to come get me to escort me back to his office. Within minutes William Wesley, our local mayor, came to meet me in the lobby, quickly ushering me down the corridor to his office. Once the door was shut securely behind us, I wasted no time asking him why he requested a meeting with me.

"Why am I here? I've paid you for the year already, William," I said, crossing my arms against my chest.

"I...I need help," he stammered.

My right foot tapped with impatience, I braced myself for the bullshit I knew was coming.

"What can I help you with?" I asked, pursing my lips together.

Chapter Nine

GIANNA

Meet My Baby Daddy

"Mom! Dad!" I screamed, barging through the front door.

Neither of them responded as I made my way to the back of their four-bedroom ranch style house. My parents purchased this house when I was about twelve when we moved here from Chicago. I was raised in this house, it held so many memories for me. Passing by the "biblical wall" in the hallway, my hand grazed the Holy Bible that sat on the home-made mantel. My father placed pictures, bronzed wooden scriptures, and metal scrapings that were pieced together along the wall in the front hallway. It was his pride and joy. Most days, he knelt on his knees in prayer and praise right here in this space.

"Gia? Darling, what are you doing here at this time of day?

Is everything alright?" my mother questioned with a concerned look on her face.

"Hi, mom, dad. I need to talk to both you," I sheepishly spoke, twisting my fingers together—something I did whenever I was nervous or anxious about something.

My father rose from his favorite chair in the sunroom to embrace me in his strong arms. The churn of my stomach made bile rise to the forefront of my throat, terrified that this would be the last hug my father would wrap me in for a long time. My parents were loving, patient, strict, God-fearing people. I knew the news I was about to burden them with would leave them shocked and in despair. Letting go of him, I quickly hugged my mother before taking a seat in front of them on the old brown leather couch.

Hunching over with my elbows on my knees, I drew a sharp breath in, closing my eyes before releasing the breath forcefully out between my lips. What I had to say to them was hard for me to come to terms with. My parents instilled *death do you part* in me, as true believers of the bible. The sanction of marriage was holy to them, but I refused to put up with William's bullshit.

"What's wrong, darling?" my father's deep voice interrupted my thoughts.

My mother reached over from her chair to his, grabbing his hand into hers. Steadying him and bracing herself for whatever I was going to unload on them.

"I'm filing for divorce from William," I exhaled.

A pause fell across the room. Both stared on, in expectation for me to keep talking, wanting to get to the root of the problem so they could convince me that counseling and prayer would cause these devilish thoughts of divorce to flee from me. I knew what was coming, but mentally I prepared for this day for almost two weeks straight. Powering through my nervousness, I sat up, straightening out my back, squaring my shoulders.

"William has a mistress; he just came back from Costa Rica with her after lying to everyone saying it was a work trip. Lying to his office that you, dad, were having major surgery, and he needed to be there to support us," I revealed.

"Baby, sometimes a man goes through these phases. It's not right, but you, as a wife, have a responsibility to bring him back around. It doesn't seem right, but every relationship has struggles. This too shall pass," my mother encouraged.

"Ma, I'm not going back. I've been the best wife I knew how to be. I've waited for him to get settled into the position, so we held off at his insistence. Over the last year, William hasn't touched me like a husband should. Always having an excuse. I've begged him to open his mind about me starting the bakery, even though the money was my own. I've begged to finally start the family I thought we both believed in. I decided to take matters in my own hands and finally stop begging for what I know I deserve. I have the paperwork for the divorce, I've rented out an apartment, and most importantly...I'm pregnant," I breathed.

The weight of my words lifted off my shoulders, evaporating in the air. My mother gasped, pulling her hand away from my father's, lifting it to her mouth. I watched as the vein in my father's forehead pulsed, a sign that things were about to get real heated.

"Explain to me how you're pregnant when you just said your husband hasn't laid a hand on you?" my father demanded, moving to the edge of his seat.

"It's not what you think, daddy. I have been completely faithful, unlike William. I went to a sperm bank, selected a donor, and had the procedure completed. I found out this morning that the IVF was successful, I'm going to be a mommy!" I revealed.

Stunned into silence, my parents looked at each other before they both began to stumble over each other's words. I could see a mixture of excitement and disappointment in my mother's face.

"What the hell is wrong with you?" my father barked, now standing over me.

I flinched back as spit left his lips, the snarl on his face was something out of a horror film. I've never seen my father this upset, especially not with me. Our relationship didn't hold many secrets, he always made me feel that I was able to talk to him about anything. His role as a pastor gave him an understanding side that was lost on so many people.

"I know this comes as a huge surprise and it will take so time to get used to the thought. But my decision is final. I pray that I have your full support in this because it will hurt me if I don't. However, I will move forward with or without you both, I just hope I don't have to," I cried.

My mother gently pushed my father out of the way, sitting down on the couch next to me, holding out her arms for me to fall in. After bawling like a baby in my mother's arms, I straightened up, slightly pushing her back. My father had long taken a seat on the arm of the chair, rubbing my back as I cried.

"Wait, there is more," I sniffled.

"Speak, my child," my father's voice boomed in my ear.

"The sperm bank made a major mistake. They gave me sperm that belonged to a man that had cancer, saving it for when he was ready to have a child. He came to the bakery after finding out where I worked. He wants to have a hands-on experience with this baby. Also, possibly wanting me to carry at least one more child for him being that I'm having his first. He's been with me every step of the way since we found out about the mix-up. He went with me to the appointment today, along with his brother and best friend. His parents don't know yet, but Jared, um his brother is Jared, wants to throw us a celebration dinner tonight. My baby's father, your grandbaby's father's name is Noah Robert's, and I'd really appreciate it if you showed up for me tonight," I gushed out.

"What?" they both yelled in unison.

"I know, I know it's a lot to take in at once. I wanted to come to you, but I knew you'd talk me out of it. I didn't want to take that chance of remaining unhappy in the life I was drowning in," I sulked.

The alarm on my father's phone signaled this conversation

was over. Glancing at the cable box, I knew it was time for their afternoon prayer session with the deacons of the church.

We all stood up at the same time, my mother the first to speak.

"Text me the address of this so-called celebration. I'll never allow you to feel alone, but I want you to understand that this conversion is far from over," she warned.

My father just grunted out a goodbye, basically dismissing me.

"Richard, grab my prayer oil out the bedroom, please. I'll meet you in the car," she ordered, moving past me as if I was invisible.

Chapter Ten

NOAH

A Family Man

I took in the decorations around the house, my stomach rumbling from the captivating smells of food coming from the kitchen. Chantel and Jared made magic happen within hours. They left me feeling extremely grateful to have them both in my life. Never in a million years would I imagine having a baby with someone other than Alana, but sometimes our plans aren't aligned with God's. And things don't add up to our vision. Sneaking into the kitchen to steal a few tastes of what chef had cooked up, Chantel caught me with a mini crab cake stuffed half-way in my mouth.

"Get out of this kitchen! This food is for the guests. Everyone should be here soon. You can wait, fat boy," she chuckled, punching me lightly in my stomach, causing me to cough.

"I'm the guest of honor, I get first dips," I grinned, now

snatching up a fried mozzarella puff tossing it in my mouth.

The puff was fresh out of the grease, burning the roof of my mouth. That's what I get for being greedy, I guess. It was good as hell and worth the burn. I don't know how chef came up with these items to serve, but he put his foot in everything he made. Even the simplest meal he made tasted like fine dining. As I reached for another one, the doorbell rang. Hiding my disappointment of not being able to finish sampling, I jogged lightly to open the door. Yelling behind me, I told chef everything was tasting great as always.

Gianna stood at the door in an all-white halter dress with her hair pinned up, with soft ringlets of curls framing her face. She was absolutely mesmerizing, leaving me speechless. All I managed to mutter out was hello. I was standing there panting like a dog in heat, with my tongue hanging out and my tail wagging. Flashing me a dazzling smile, Gianna sidestepped out the frame to show that she had her parents with her.

"Noah, this is my father, Richard and my mother, Giselle," she introduced them both.

Returning the smile, I introduced myself to her parents, ushering them into the house.

"Wow, Jared's house is beautiful. These decorations are very nice. How'd they set this up so last minute?" Gianna asked, checking out the surroundings.

"So, this isn't your house, Noah?" Ms. Giselle questioned.

"No, ma'am, this is my brother's house. He is the one throwing the celebration for us," I confirmed.

Slowly, her parents nodded their heads, and we ventured deeper into the living area. As we passed the kitchen, I told them to grab a plate so they can get started on the appetizers. I offered the different drink options we had while they were expressing how good everything looked. It was easy to tell that Mr. Richard rarely missed a meal. His potbelly stuck out farther than it should under his shirt. I'm sure with being a pastor, he always had cakes, pies, and hearty Sunday dinners thrown at him by his church members. Out of the corner of my eye, I peeped that Gianna had removed herself to the edge of the kitchen, seemingly allowing her parents to get what they want first. Picking up a plate for her, I held out my hand for her to join us in the kitchen. Lord knows it was more than enough space. Jared told me to build this place for entertaining, so that's exactly what I did. This was a gourmet chef's dream kitchen, even though Jared can't even boil water.

Extending my hand behind me, I motioned for Gianna to come to me.

"Gia, come show me what you want so I can make you a plate," I ordered, resisting the urge to pull her body into mine.

Jared and Chantel made their entrance from the stairs behind the kitchen.

"Noah, I know you are not still sneaking food before the guests arrive," Chantel hollered from the stairs.

"The company has arrived, and I'm making sure they eat, so ah-ha," I teased, sticking out my tongue at Chantel.

Hurriedly rushing down the rest of the stairs, they greeted

our guests with apologizes for not being available when they first arrived. Jared hugged Gianna tightly, telling me to put a rush on the plate I was making for her. After awkwardly shaking hands with both Gianna's parents, Jared told everyone to come sit in the dining room to get to know each other. Before we even left the kitchen, Mr. Richard doubled back to get a refill of the mini appetizers.

"It's good, ain't it?" I chuckled, plucking another mozzarella ball off the little round spoon it was placed on.

"Umm-hmm," was his only reply as he stuffed his mouth.

No sooner than we sat down, a quick ringing of the doorbell alerted us that we had more visitors arriving. Knowing it was my parents, because we had not invited anyone else, I yelled for them to grab a plate and meet us in the dining room. It was showtime. I wasn't sure if Gianna had already warned her parents why we would here, but I hadn't said a word to my parents. Nervousness began to set in, I wasn't sure how my parents were going to react to this news.

"Hey, everybody. The party has arrived!" my mother boasted, sliding into the dining room doing a little two step.

"Hey, ma, where's dad?" I asked, glancing behind her.

"He's still in the kitchen eating the food before he makes a plate. You know the usual," she cackled.

"Don't be in here talking trash, Vic," his deep baritone filled the room.

Smacking her on the butt, he pulled out a chair for her then took a seat right next to her.

"Oh hello, everyone," my mother smiled, glancing at Jared

and I with confusion etched in her face.

"Gia?"

I locked eyes with her, waiting for her approval to speak. Gianna shifted her weight in the chair. Clutching her hand over her heart, she nodded a non-verbal yes.

"Well, mom, dad...you know that last year I had cancer, which caused me to freeze my sperm," I started, taking my time.

"Yes, we also know it has cleared, which we are grateful to God for. What is it that you need to tell us?" my mother demanded.

"Give him a second, Ma," Jared spoke up.

"Wait, where is Alana?" my father asked.

"We can talk about that in just a moment. I know everyone is anxious, so let me just spit this out. Please," I pleaded.

"Long story short, Chantel's co-worker made a mistake sending Gianna my sperm instead of the sperm she selected. Risking her job, she provided us with the information on Gianna to locate her. I'd never want to have a child out there wasn't in my life. We meet Gianna at the IVF doctor today, where they confirmed that she is indeed pregnant," I paused to allow everything I said sink in.

"Wait a minute! Are you playing with me, boy?" my mom hollered across the table.

"No ma'am. This is Gianna, the mother of your first grandchild. These are her parents, Mr. Richard and Mrs. Giselle," I answered giddily.

Once the initial shock wore off, my parents were so excited they didn't know what to do with themselves. Chef Lance came into the dining area to ask if we were ready for the main course while sliding around a server on wheels that we choose more drinks from. Everything seemed to be going well. Everyone was making small talk getting to know each other. The mothers were already making plans to get together to go baby shopping.

The meal arrived prompting Pastor Richard to ask us to join hands, bowing our heads for the prayer over our dinner. In the middle of the prayer, the doorbell rang over and over, causing him to rush through it.

"Amen," we all called at the end.

Jared leaped from the table with an attitude, laboring to the door to see who was on the other side.

"Alana, we are having a private moment," he persisted as I was walking up behind him to see who was ringing his doorbell like a madman.

Rushing past him to get to me, Alana barged into the foyer, demanding to know why I haven't been home in a week.

"Alana, we both know the answer to that. The condo is now yours; I have changed everything into your name. You will never be homeless, but I'm done. We're done. It's not up for decision," I stated sadly.

"Noahhhhhhhhhh, you don't mean thatttttttt!" she screamed, clenching my shirt in her hands.

My mother rounded the corner leading the pack to get to the bottom of what was going on in the foyer where Jared and

I were. My embarrassment grew once I realized the only person that didn't follow her was Chef Lance.

"What the hell is going on out here?" my mom questioned.

"Mrs. Victoria, Noah hasn't come home in over a week! He blocked me from calling him, hasn't called me, and I need answers!" Alana yelled.

'Lana, first, I suggest you lower your voice when you are addressing me. Second, I know damn well Rochelle raised you better than this to barge into someone's home, causing a damn scene. I'm sure it's more to the story, but now isn't the time. We have company. You and Noah can discuss whatever y'all have going on later," my mom scolded.

"Can everyone go back to the dining room, please? I promise this won't take long," I damn near begged.

"I'm staying until we work this out, No. I miss you," Alana claimed, gently touching my arm.

Scoffing, I jerked my arm back from her grasp. I swear it felt like her fingertips burned me to the bone.

"Maybe we should just go," Gianna wheezed.

"No, just give me a few minutes alone, please," I stated.

"Yeah, maybe you should just go," Alana spat Gianna's words back to her.

Staring me dead in the face, Alana asked me who the hell Gianna was. The way Mr. Richard peered at me, I knew I needed to tread very lightly. I felt the color drain from my face, humiliated that the celebration swiftly went downhill. As Alana stepped deeper into the house, my father told everyone to retreat to the dining room to finish dinner before the food got cold.

Patting me on the back, he whispered, "Handle this, son."

Once the foyer was empty of everyone but Alana and I, she began to grovel.

"I know I fucked up, No, but we will get past this like we do everything else. Please just come home so I can fix this, baby," she pleaded.

An accidental snort left my nose, the laughter at her suggestion came from the very pit of my stomach. My head flung back; tears stung my eyes. For a moment I couldn't catch my breath, I laughed so hard. The audacity of her to allow the thought of rekindling our relationship to cross her narrow ass mind. Ain't no fucking way she was serious right now.

"Alana, there isn't an "us" anymore. We are through. Done. It's no coming back from this shit. Even after the blatant disrespect of getting pregnant by another nigga, and paying for the abortion with my fucking money, you still decided to embarrass us both by showing your ass in the hood. I know damn well you didn't think I was that soft, to take your ass back! As my mother said, we have company right now. Please see your way out the door," I sneered.

"Nigga, I loved you through everything. Don't stand here and act like you never cheated. We've been down this road too many times to count! So, no, this is not the end of the road for us."

"I've never ran up in no bitch raw. Ever. I've never had to

make a chick get an abortion. This is not the road we've been down before, Alana!"

"It was an accident, Noah! Damn!" she cursed.

"You're right about that part, Alana. You picked one of Jared's never amount to nothing else corner boys to fuck up your happy home," I gritted.

"Excuse me, sorry to interrupt, but can you direct me to the nearest restroom, please?" Gianna requested her voice dripping with extra sweetness.

Locking eyes with her, I knew she only came out to check on me. I tucked my bottom lip in to hide my smile.

"Yes, of course," I assured her.

"Who did you say this was?" Alana snapped.

"I didn't. But if you must know, Gianna is the mother of my child. The pregnancy has been confirmed. And you interrupted our celebration with your bullshit," I countered.

"So, just that fast you have her prancing around her like she's family? This bitch ain't royalty!" Alana screamed.

Not even giving her the satisfaction of an argument, Gianna held her head high with a smirk while waiting for me to escort her to the bathroom.

"See yourself out, Lana. We're done here," I announced.

Without giving Alana the chance to give a rebuttal, I turned my back to her, walking down the hall with Gianna. After quietly apologizing to Gianna over the bullshit that had taken place during what was supposed to be our celebration, I told her I'd meet her back in the dining room.

The loud squealing caught everyone off guard. What the

hell happened? We all jumped up, racing to the sound of the noise. Right as we reached the hallway, we saw Alana trying to overpower Gianna to get her to the ground. I yelled for Alana to stop, rushing towards them, but before I could get there, Gianna had knocked Alana's ass out with a two-jab combo. Damn, my little pastor's kid had hands. Mrs. Giselle raced to Gianna to make sure she was okay. Alana awkwardly made it off the floor, not ready to give up the fight. Out the corner of my eye, I saw Alana snatch the glass sculpture off the mantel, aiming for Gianna's head. Before my legs reached her to knock it out her hand, Mrs. Giselle turned just in time to hit Alana with a nasty uppercut, causing her to crumble to the ground. Everyone gasped in shock.

"I wasn't always the pastor's wife, I was born and raised on the South Side of Chicago. Play with me," she threatened.

"I'm so, so sorry. This is not how our night was supposed to go," I apologized after making sure Gianna was okay.

"Let's get out of here," Mr. Richard commanded.

"Get your sister out of here too, yo," Jared said to Chantel.

Chantel helped Alana out the floor, guiding her to the door. With each step Alana took, she screamed that it wasn't over, I'd always belong to her. If I didn't think she was crazy before, it was cemented in my mind now. No one said a word as Chantel lead her out of our view, and we heard the door shut. Suddenly, my mother spoke up.

"Son, you need to keep an eye on that one."

Chapter Eleven

WILLIAM

Damn

The office was buzzing with excitement, the President of the United States confirmed he would attend my Mayor's Ball in a few months. This was by far the largest honor any government official in Ohio has ever received. Almost instantly, upon receiving the news, the tickets began to fly off the websites. We had six months to create the most extravagant ball the state has ever seen. My team was brainstorming on ideas and different themes for that evening. Securing myself ten extra tickets, I wanted to make sure I had a VIP table for my own family and friends. Currently, my focus was on getting my wife back, making sure she was standing tall by my side on that night and every night from here on out.

"I'm going to my wife's shop to get some breakfast. Do

you want me to bring you back anything?" I asked walking past my secretary.

"Yes, some tea, please! It doesn't matter what you bring back, everything she makes is delicious," she smiled.

Bypassing the line wrapped around the corner, I flexed a little when the person in line scoffed when I slid through the door.

"This is my spot; my wife and I own it. I'm not skipping the line," I smirked.

It amazed me how quickly her shop took off. It normally takes a smaller business a long time to pick up steam if it ever does. The smell inside the bakery was heavenly, with the aroma of warm strawberries and honey. So many times, I'd walk through the door after a long day at work, this smell is what greeted me. My niece Dana noticed me first, wobbling her obese body from behind the counter to give me a quick hug.

The rest of the employees acknowledged me with a hello, or a nod. Offering a quick nod and hand wave in return, I hurried to the back, knowing Gianna would be in the kitchen prepping. Once my eyes drunk in her vision, my body reacted to the sight of her. She had her back to me, pounding on some dough rolling and forming it in the shape she wanted to achieve. The rhythm of her rolling took over her body, her backside shaking with each pound she delivered to the dough. Getting caught up in the show she was unwittingly providing, I licked my lips, advancing on her close enough to attack her neck with kisses.

Out of sheer surprise, she elbowed me hard to the ribs before turning around to smack me. Startled, I threw my arms up to defend myself. Who did she think I was? She'd only been away from our home for a week and some change. My face darkened in anger, she had to know it was me. Even if she was still upset with me, she didn't have to resort to physical assault. Hell, I was the mayor. What if someone saw this? How would that look?

"It's just me, baby, damn," I scoffed.

"I'm not your baby, don't put your infested lips on me. I don't know where they've been," she snidely replied.

"Whatever, Gia. I'm not going to have this argument with you here. I missed you, so I came here to see your face to face. I'm still your husband, come home tonight, so we can talk," I persisted.

Without giving so much as an eye roll, Gianna turned her back to me. Hating to be ignored, I whistled through my teeth, blowing off some of my frustration. Gianna was testing my patience. As the head of the household, I always expected her to submit to me. Her father taught the submission of wives to husbands the first time I ever visited their church. When I saw her singing in the choir, I just knew I had to have her. Beautiful, voice of an angel, body bodacious enough to give them hell, and a pastor's daughter. What the Lord delivered in my lap that day, was nothing less than the perfect woman. Yes, I cheated on her, but she was my queen. Innocent, timid but willing to please. However, the things I was into I could never expose her to.

"William, I am working. Did you miss the line around the corner? I am busy. We are busy. If you are getting something, fine, get it, and see yourself out. Please and thank you," she scolded.

"Walk me out to the front with a smile, I'll grab what I want and go. But tonight, I'd appreciate it if you were there on time for dinner so we can talk, Gia," I said, gently wiping flour dust off her cheek.

The wheels in Gianna's head were churning, it was obvious she was weighing her options. Propping my chin up on both hands, I blinked my eyes innocently. We both knew it was in her best interest to agree to my terms. Otherwise, my stubborn ass wasn't leaving any time soon.

"Fine," she hissed.

I smirked, knowing she was going to give in because she was serious about making sure everything was done on time and correctly. On the way towards the front, I smacked her ass, admiring the way it jiggled like jello. Damn, I loved this woman. She turned around, abruptly putting up her fist as a warning. She had always been against public affection, but I didn't care; she belonged to me.

"Hey, baby."

A voice sounding just like Sydney's called out. My eyes never left the options in the case. Picking out a Crème Brulee danish and a French toast muffin, I lifted my head from the case to find Sydney perched on the other side of the glass. Instantly, my head started spinning.

"You want some tea, Unc?" Dana asked.

"Yes, what options are on today's menu?"

"William baby, get me an herbal honey tea," Sydney sung.

Out the corner of my eye, I saw Gianna's body go rigid. Everything seemed to move in slow motion as Gianna arched her back, twisting her body to face Sydney. I swallowed hard. While I've never seen Gia get confrontational, I wasn't dumb. Even the sweetest woman had her limits.

"Sydney, don't do this. Stop with the disrespect while you are ahead," I muttered.

"Put a lease on your bitch," Gianna roared.

"It's not like that, baby I promise," I swore, waving Sydney off with my free hand.

When the next customer was called, Sydney stepped to the side of the line hands planted firmly on her hips. Anxious to end this feud before it started, I sidestepped past the employees that were still taking and preparing orders. All eyes were on me, it was like everyone was anticipating my next move.

"You are mine, my man now. She left you, William. She's trying to get pregnant by another man, but you are here in her presence like we haven't been together for over a year. I'm tired of hiding. For the last almost weeks, we've been waking up next to each other, and I'm not going back to sneaking around!" Sydney screamed.

"You will not disrespect my WIFE in her place of business! Take your shit and get back to the office!" I hollered.

Sydney stood firm in defiance. Her face was drawn tight, signifying she wasn't moving.

"Now!" I commanded, raising my voice.

Sydney blew me a kiss, telling me she'd see me at the office.

Gianna smacked the shit out of me. My face stung so bad I knew I'd have a bruise. Sydney told her to never put her hands on me again, or she'd have to deal with her. Before I knew about what was coming, Gianna jumped in front of me, punching Sydney dead in the mouth. Blood flew everywhere, parts of me wanted to see what Sydney would do next, but I knew I had to break this up right now. Pushing Gianna behind me protectively, I firmly demanded Sydney to leave.

Sydney gripped my face tightly with her delicate hand causing my lips to make an "O" shape. Spitting the blood from her mouth to mine, she laughed, kissing me deeply. Stunned, I froze. My dick bricked up. Every part of me wanted to bend her ass over in the middle of this bakery, not caring who was watching. The problem was all eyes were already on us. I had to get out of there. Without another word, she strutted to the door, knowing I'd follow like the freak that I was.

Chapter Twelve

ALANA

Warning

Imagine walking into a celebration dinner for your man's baby, but you aren't the one pregnant. Everyone laughing and joking like shit was cool. Families intertwined that didn't even know each other a week before. That shit still wasn't sitting well with me, I was determined to get more information on this chick. Yes, I knew the donor's office fucked up, but since I wasn't the one carrying his seed, he should've let that bastard child go. When I found out that I fucked up but getting pregnant by Rico's fine, irresistible ass, I went straight to the chop shop. I didn't mean to get caught out there, though. Noah was taking this break-up thing too damn far.

"You hungry, shorty?" Rico asked, breaking through my thoughts.

"Starving, actually," I spoke.

"Good. Go make us something to eat. Don't let your man starve, that's in the keep a man rule book," he grinned before inhaling the smoke from his blunt.

It was hard to distinguish if the smoke had his eyes set that low already, or if he was giving me the seductive, bedroom eyes. He was good for casting a spell on me with. His lips curled up in a teasing smile, as I pushed up from the bed to go see what there was to cook in the kitchen. Even though I was making my way back into Noah's good graces to win my man back, I was still slumming it with Rico until I figured out how to get him to come home. The vibe between Rico and I was electrifying, the gangsta in him was alluring as hell. Some kind of way, it just drew me to him, Noah had swag, but he wasn't a street nigga like Jared and Rico. Back in the day, I wanted Jared so bad, but he wasn't checking for me more than sliding down my throat. So instead, I started checking for his younger brother.

"It's nothing in here, bae," I shouted to the back room.

"Go get something then," Rico responded.

I hated this side of him, I'm used to being catered to. Noah always made sure we had food in the house. If I wanted something that wasn't in the house to eat, he'd order out or go get it. Rico's house stayed dirty with people running in and out. Even the few times I did clean up, by the next day, there were blunt guts and liquor bottles everywhere. These muthafuckas were the gutter of the gutter, but if I wanted to play my role in his life, I knew not to complain too much just yet.

"Why don't you order us something to eat?" I whined, stomping my feet like a toddler.

Rico appeared in the kitchen so fast it scared me. Huffing hard, fists balled up by his sides, the vein in his forehead was pulsing. Rico's temper had always been easy to trigger a violent reaction in him. I rolled my eyes, watching the rise and fall of his chest. How dare he be upset with me because I told him to order us something to eat. Shit, he was the one that asked if I was hungry anyway. The devil danced around in his eyes; it was the quiet before the storm. We stood off against each other in the tiny kitchen. Frustrated, I blew air from between my lips attempting to move past him.

Smack!

Paralyzed by fear, I froze. In that moment, Rico looked like the Hulk compared to my petite frame. Breaking out of my trance, I started to wail on him with all my might. No match for his strength, he lifted me by my neck. My feet dangled in the air, as he slammed me into the grease and grim filled wall. Soundlessly, I sobbed not wanting to use too much oxygen. Strategically positioning my legs in front of me, I kicked him with all I had, causing him to double over. Wounded, he dropped my body to the floor like I was a rag doll. He backed up, crunched over, holding himself with both hands.

"Bitch, what you do that dumb shit for?" he cursed.

"You were going to kill me," I choked out.

Collapsing next to me, Rico grabbed me by my hair, pulling me closer to him. I flinched waiting for the next wave of violence; my whole body tensed up. Rico surprised me by gently kissing my temple, whispering that he was sorry. My face ached from the backhand he hit me with, I knew it would leave a bruise. The only thing running across my mind was that Noah had never put his hands on me. He just wasn't that type of man, their father raised them right. Rico, on the other hand, was raised by the streets. His heart was so cold he sold dope to his own mother. He once told me that either way she was going to buy it, so why not make money off her. She stopped caring about him and his sister years ago. Her family traveled around the hood like a pack of zombies. Soulless. He wasn't even sure if she knew what he looked like anymore.

"Lana, I'm sorry. For real, yo. I have all this rage in me, I won't hit you again," he promised.

Immediately accepting his apology, I laid there next to him with my mind telling me to run. Rico slid his body over mine, holding himself up on one arm, which was planted next to my ear. His pink lips were so close to my face, but still not touching me. My stomach tightened, I just had to have him. Pulling him closer, I sucked his lips into mine biting the bottom one. He groaned, then his stomach rumbled. I laughed. Hard.

"Let me order some food, bae," I cackled, pushing him off me.

"Yeah, you do that. I'm going to go back in the bedroom to finish playing my game," he said, helping me up from the kitchen floor.

Rico dusted the dirt off my back, cuffing my butt before

smacking it. I did a little shake for him, letting him past me. My body landed hard on the old, tattered couch. I was sure that this dingy, saggy cushion couch had been in this pathetic apartment. It wasn't a night that I've ever spent here, and I didn't see it on the horizon.

Folding my body into a more comfortable position, which was hard to do anywhere in his space, I sat with my back towards the bedroom door. After ordering us some pizza, with extra cheese and pepperoni, I scrolled through Instagram, seeing what was going on out there with my friends today. One post caught my eye, it was on my sister's page. She was eating some type of donut, acting like it was the best thing she has ever eaten. Chantel called it delectable, moaning while chewing. Reading the comments of how good this bakery was, I decided I might need to check it out. Just as I was moving on to something else, someone typed that Gianna was the best. That's when it hit me, Chantel was advertising Noah's bitch ass baby momma. My blood began to boil, where was the loyalty?

After I googled the address for the bakery, I shot Tina a quick text letting her know I needed her help tonight. The bubbles appeared on my screen, without a delay. My bestie hit me back asking how to dress for the occasion. Smiling, I sent back a text informing her she needed to be in all black, preferably something covering her face. Tonight, we were going to fuck Two Sweets up. Sooner or later, this bitch needed to learn that Noah belongs to me. It felt as though in a blink of an eye, she turned my man, his family, and my sister against me. I didn't like the way Noah was protective of her already. I hoped she was a quick learner because I wasn't letting him go at any cost.

"Gurl, Noah's little accidental sperm carrying chick owns this bakery that we are going to trash. I think the ugly bitch is after my man! I'm not having it. You know Noah belongs to me and only me," I rumbled into the speaker of my iPhone.

Just leaving Rico's apartment, I sped off to my condo to hurry up to shower and change into fighting gear. Already knowing what I was going to throw on, I mapped out how to tear up Gianna's place without us getting caught in my mind. I knew a few crackheads around Tina's way that were still halfway functioning and were always renting out their cars to get money for dope. I asked Tina to go outside to hunt at least one of them down, so we can use a car that wasn't going to link back to either of us. In case she had cameras instilled around the building. It was in a nicer area of town, so I knew even if her shop didn't, the others around it certainly would.

Tina secured the hooptie we needed to make the mad dash to Gianna's place. When 10 p.m. hit, I arrived. Tina's secured the car by paying him upfront with just enough extra for him not to care how long we kept the car. Barely waiting for him to scurry off into the darkness, I pulled off. The car was filthy, we had to brush the trash in the floor to even be able to sit in it. Even with the gloves I had on, I didn't want to touch the steering wheel. The odor was so pungent I wasn't sure if I'd ever be able to get it out of my nose.

"I love when we ride out on some grimy shit!" Tina exclaimed.

"Me too, but in this case, I wish we didn't have to. However, I feel in my soul she is going to come for my man. And I can't have that. Noah Roberts is mine, always has been, always will be," I lectured.

"Gurllll, you ain't gotta tell me! I know! But shit, if you had snagged Jared's fine ass, we'd be laid up in the shade with a chef and that huge house of his," she commented.

'You know I tried to ruin his life with this pussy, but he refused to take the bait. His fine ass had too many options at the time," I shrugged.

"Yeah, well, you got the next best thing. Noah fine as shit too, sis. And the way he has you living ain't nothing to complain about. Even when he's mad at you, he provides for you. I still can't believe he transferred the condo into your name," this dizzy bitch said, like she didn't already know I was the shit.

Parking around the back of the building, a few stores down next to the other side of the dumpster, we stepped out the car with a bag of cleaning supplies just in case any store owners were still hanging around we'd look like a cleaning crew. What wasn't visible was the hammers we had hidden in our jackets. The thrill of destroying someone's property rushed through my veins. We made our way around to the front of the bakery. From the outside, even in the dark, it looked pretty upscale.

After a double take ensured that no one was lurking in the

area but us. Swiftly, I unzipped my jacket, snatching the hammer from the pocket it was in. Tina followed suit, and together we smashed the glass of the window. Tina used her elbow, pushing some of the shattered glass in so we were able to jump in the store quickly. An alarm went off, so we knew we only had a few minutes before getting caught. Hurriedly we went to the tables, breaking them in half with the hammer since they were wooden. Knocking everything over in the path, back out the window we ran, laughing all the way back to the car. Once we reached the car, I peeled off as fast as the hooptie allowed. We heard the sirens coming in the other direction, I saw the flashing lights approaching, but they stopped right in front of the store as we cruised back to Tina's hood. What a beautiful night this had become.

Chapter Thirteen

CHANTEL

The Drama

*A*nother busy day at the office. The last client I had spent more time flirting or trying to flirt, I should say than getting the imperative information I was providing. It was so many people on the schedule for today, I just hoped the rest of the day breezed by. Jared promised to bring me lunch but refused to tell me what he was bringing. Secretly, I hoped it was something that Chef Lance prepared. His food was better than anything I've ever tasted in my life.

The messenger on my computer went off, my boss was asking to see me in his office. My boss was a pretty cool and laid-back guy, but most of the time, when he summons me to his office, it was because he needed me to pick up someone else's workload along with mine. Every nurse was in place today, so I wondered what he needed. Whatever he needed, I'd just suck it up and roll with it.

Knocking on the side of the door, since he had it open, I stepped in.

"Hey, Anthony. You needed to see me?" I questioned.

"Yes, Chantel. Shut the door and take a seat please," he insisted.

Surprised, that he told me to take a seat I did as he asked. He normally leaves the door open when he calls me in the office.

"What's up?"

Sighing heavily, he responded, "I received a call last evening just as I was leaving the office. It was shocking, to say the least. I've weighed my options with my boss, and the legal board," he informed.

Choking on my spit, I started coughing uncontrollably. My throat began to burn, my eyes followed suit as the tears welled in my eyes. I knew where this was going, but I couldn't wrap my mind around who made the call into the office. Anthony slid from behind his desk, coming to take a seat next to me in the open chair. Placing a hand on my back, he asked if I was okay.

"Who called you?" I stammered out.

"Your sister, Alana Man. She told me everything. Pamela will be released after our conversation. Honestly, I'm beyond disappointed that you were involved in this situation. But on the human standpoint, I get it. I really do. This is your family. You wanted to protect them at all costs. You wanted to be the bearer of bad news, and it seems you wanted to protect Pam and the company. But what you did was, as you already know, illegal and unethical, Chantel."

"I know. I can't even say anything other than what you already said. I'm sorry, I know I will have to accept any punishment given. I understand that this could cause me to lose my job and license," I sobbed.

"Well, after speaking with a few higher-ups, because this is your family, we won't reach out to the board. But you will be suspended for two weeks without pay. Please leave the building after this conversation and really take the time to think about what could've happened. We cannot allow this to happen again. At all," he spoke sternly.

"Yes, sir, thank you. Again, I sincerely apologize. I'll clear my desk and see you in two weeks."

"No, don't clear your desk. I don't want anyone asking questions. If anyone asks, you had a family emergency. Got it?" he asked, patting my back firmly like he was burping a baby.

Seeing me to the door, he told me to go straight to my desk to get my stuff to leave for the door. It wasn't stated but understood that I was not to stop by Pam's desk to speak to her or give her a head's up. Most of the other nurses and agents were with a client, so it made it easy for me to sneak out without everyone trying to figure out why I was leaving.

Once I made it to my car, I was livid. How dare Alana do some foul as shit like this to me? I almost lost my damn job. I worked hard as hell for my degree. Not saying she didn't, but she didn't use her degree, she depends on Noah to take care of her. She felt like working was beneath her. This bitch was going to catch these hands, it was no other way around it. Everything in me wanted to break down and cry, but the anger inside me stopped the tears from coming.

Dialing my mother to tell her what her hateful, miserable daughter did, my phone rang in my hand before the call connected.

"Hello?"

"Umm, it's Gianna. If you can...if you aren't busy..." she stuttered.

Frustrated, not by her, but the way my morning was going, I snapped into the phone.

"Spit it out. What you need, Gianna?"

"Umm, sorry to bother you. Never mind," she cried.

Instantly, regret took over my body. My next words went to the dead air since Gianna hung up in my ear. My shoulders slumped, calling her right back to see what she needed. It wasn't fair of me to take my attitude out on her. She didn't answer my calls after I dialed her back three times. Busting an illegal U-Turn, I headed towards her shop, hoping that was where she was.

My breathing felt constricted when I pulled up to the bakery. The shop was in disarray and a camera crew perched outside trying to shoot their story of vandalism. Damn. Here she was calling me because she needed a shoulder, and instead, I gave her my ass to kiss in my tone. Suddenly, looking at all the damage, my mind went straight to Alana. My heart spoke to me saying she was the culprit. This was right up her trifling ass alley. Pushing past the people outside chattering and making assumptions, I stepped into the bakery calling out for Gianna.

"Gia!" I shouted throughout the chaos.

An employee pointed to the back of the store, letting me know where to find her. Allowing the guy to walk past me with a table over his back, I scooted behind him, my head searching in each direction for Gianna. From a few feet ahead of me, I heard soft sniffling, which let me know I was close to finding her.

"Gia, I'm here."

There was intense sobbing now.

"Gia," I paused.

Inaudible words left her mouth, she was balled up in a corner with her arms wrapped tightly around her knees. Her head nestled down firmly down over her arms. It pained me to see her this way. I barely knew her, but her spirit was so calming and pure. Seeing her this way made me want to run up on Alana this very moment.

"Stand up, I got you," I mumbled, holding my arms out.

She lifted herself slowly from the ground, the agony wearing on her face clear as day. Her eyes were bloodshot, her face showed a hurt that I wasn't exactly sure came from her store being damaged.

"I'm sorry that I bothered you, there was no need for you to come all the way here. I'm good. Thanks though," she foolishly apologized.

"Gia, I owe you the apology. When you called, I had just

gotten suspended for two weeks without pay from my sister calling my boss about the baby and the mix up about the sperm. Well, now, the baby. It had nothing at all to do with you. I'm sorry that I was so harsh. I'm pissed at her, not you. That's why I'm here, you didn't deserve that," I countered.

Sadness took over her face again, the reality of what I just revealed to her hit hard. How embarrassing is it that your own sister tried to get you fired for something that was out of your control. The way Alana was handling all of this had me confused as hell. The leg she had to stand on went out the door when she got pregnant by Rico. Why she wanted to make everyone's life around her miserable was beyond my comprehension.

"Do they know who did this? It may have been Alana, and I'd understand if you pressed charges," I whispered.

"No, I doubt it was Alana. Can we talk outside in my car?"

"Lead the way."

Dumbfounded, I sat in the car listening to Gia run down the public disrespect her husband's girlfriend served in the middle of her store yesterday. My jaw hung open so wide, listening to her story. When she finished, the mood was bleak. Little did I know she wasn't finished. Quietly, she handed me her phone pressing play on a video that she received this morning from an unknown number. Sounds of lust and love-making filled the car, as tears streamed down her cheeks all over again.

"Who is this? Please don't tell me it's your husband with another woman."

"I wish I could."

"She doesn't show his face, probably because he's in a powerful position, but that is indeed him," she remarked.

"She stooped this low to send you this trash? Do you think he knows she sent it? Are you sure it's him?" I blurted.

"We've been married for years, I know every part of his body. Plus, it's hard to miss that tattoo of my name right where his heart is...well used to be," she said solemnly.

Shit, maybe Alana didn't tear up the bakery, but it surely seemed like something her and her ugly minion Tina would do. Gia had two unruly bitches coming for her neck at once; this shit was crazy. My phone vibrated in my hand, mimicking a heartbeat, so I knew it was Jared. A slight smile adorned my face. Truth be told, I never stopped loving him. He was asking me what time he needed to be there to eat lunch with me. Being very vague, I avoided dishing the drama because I didn't want him to call me while I was still in the car with Gianna. Simply, I told him I'd come to the house today for lunch because I got off early. After squaring away a time, I turned my undivided attention back to Gia, who was just sitting there staring into space.

"Hey, on some real shit...fuck that bitch, fuck your husband, and fuck Alana. You do not need this stress, don't let them see you sweat. You have to remain stress free for my niece or nephew. If you need to cry some more, we can sit out here until you get it all out. But know when we walk through those doors again, you have to put your crown on again, and move like the queen you are," I encouraged.

"Let's go then. Thank you for coming to my recuse. I'd still be crying on the floor, alone," she spoke.

"We family now, boo. Shit, after I talk to my mom, I might be allowed to trade you for Alana. Let's go clean up everything and make sure you'll be ready for service tomorrow. The show must go on," I sang to lighten the mood.

After helping with everything I possibly could, I left to meet Jared at the house for lunch. On the way there, I called my mother to tell her the latest piece of selfishness of the child she pushed out. My mother sent me to voicemail, sending me a text letting me know she was still at work, but she would call me when she got off. Glancing at the time, my face scrunched in confusion because she was normally off by now. Before I was able to send a text to respond, she sent a follow-up text letting me know she had been working doubles all week.

"Gotcha. Don't forget to call me, Mommy," I sent.

Chapter Fourteen

JARED

Rules to this Shit

The mayor hit my line again for the third time today. This nigga was about to get on my last fucking nerve. I already promised him I'd give the next two years money upfront today. Shit, if he continued to blow me up, he was going to catch this fade and not get the money. I didn't know what other illegal shit this fool was into, but his problems were the least of my worries. He better chill the fuck out.

"Yo," I annoyedly barked into the phone.

"Sorry to interrupt your day, boss. I know you're busy. I wasn't sure what time you were stopping through my office, and I have an emergency with my wife. I'm on my way to her right now. Just giving a head's up and needed to see if we could meet later or another day this week? If that's not asking for too much," he spoke.

"Nah, it's good, my G. Is your wife okay?" I sincerely inquired.

"She'll live, but she's not okay if that makes sense. Oh, by the way, the President of the United States is honoring me with his attendance to my ball in November. I have some extra tickets, I'd be glad to give you some for you and your family," he offered.

"Man, my mom will lose her mind being in the same building rubbing elbows with that type of crowd. Count me in. How many tickets can you let go? It'd be five of us," I questioned.

"Five? Cool, I'll make sure to get them to you once we link up. How about Friday?"

"I'll be there at noon."

We disconnected the call. I went from about to cuss his ass out to being excited to call my mother, giving her the exciting news about the ball. Not needing to meet up with William freed up some time in my schedule. Deciding to go check on my crews, I rode through each development. Everything was working smoothly until I got to Rico's area. This was one of the bagging spots. He was supposed to have four people with him breaking down the work and bagging it up. We just received a new shipment last night, but when I pulled up, these dumb niggas were outside, sitting on their cars, drinking and dancing around entertaining these sad looking bitches.

They were so caught up in trying to be that nigga, they never noticed that I was on the scene. Putting in a call to my other team to come pick up the work from this area, I was shutting these goofy muthafuckas down today. Music blasted through the air, the bass knocking from each old school ride that was lined up in the front of the building. What really pissed me off was that even the muscle men were outside chillin', and smoking like my product wasn't upstairs unprotected.

Anger coursed through my veins. The rules that were set in place for new shipments were not to be broken. They knew it was rules and levels to this shit. But everybody wanted to play with my damn emotions. Don't fuck with my money, my family, or my bitch, the order didn't matter. At first, I decided that I'd stay in the car watching the scene until my other crew pulled up to get my work. The longer I sat, the more heated I became. Strapping up, I jumped out the car shutting down the party with three shots in the air. The skanks ran for cover, a couple of the dudes ducked, scrambling for cover themselves. Guns were pointed at me before realizing who I was.

"Oh shit, J-Black," I heard someone shout.

"What's up, Black?" Rico called out, walking up to me, trying to dap me up.

"Why are you out here fucking party when my shit upstairs needing to be worked?"

"Nah, it's not like that, Black. We about to get started on that shit now, my dude."

He grinned like shit was really all good, showing all his fucking teeth. Which pissed me off even more. I ain't never been a dick-rider, and this muthafucka worked for me, not the other way around. Slamming my Glock in his grill, I knocked some of his teeth down his throat. Blood squirted everywhere, running down his chin; it even splashed on my fresh white T.

The rest of the crew damn near ran over each other, trying to get upstairs to not be embarrassed in front of the hood. Crazy thing was if they were just doing what they were getting racks to do, everything would be everything. My moves were rarely announced unless I called to say I needed a certain thing by a certain time. It made me question how many times they left my shit unprotected to front in the same dingy ass hood they lived in all their lives. Being the fair person I was, I made sure these niggas ate good. Each of them made more than enough money to raise up outta the gutter and stay out. However, I never asked what they did with their money. Out of everyone I put on, only a few got in and out. I respected the hell out of those men, it wasn't on no funny shit they just wanted better and finally had the means to supply it.

"Yo, Black, my bad. For real. We just wanted to relax a little bit before breaking down the work," Quinton cowered as I stepped into the room.

"Y'all can relax all you want. I'm taking my shit. I'm done, find another nigga to get bread with," I revealed.

"Come on, Black. We won't fuck up again, real shit," Stone promised.

"I know. And if you do, it's cool; you'll have to take that up with whoever you work for. Not me," I answered.

"This is extreme. Nothing is missing, and we can get it

done super quick. Don't take the food out our mouths, yo. For real," Quinton grunted.

"You took the food out of your mouths; I'll pay you for what you've done so far. But my crew will be here in a couple of minutes to get all my shit."

"Fuck this shit, you gone give us a fair one, Black!" Stone shouted, jumping up from the couch blunt hanging out his mouth advancing towards me.

My tool spit a bullet right through the middle of his forehead, midstride. Just as his body hit the floor, my other crew entered the apartment guns drawn. We locked eyes, they nodded to me nonverbally asking if I was good. A slight head nod to the dead body on the floor, I shook my head in disgust. Rico came running into the apartment to see what happened. His right-hand man laid out in the middle of the living room caused tears to come to his eyes, but he knew better to utter a word. Explaining to him what I already informed the rest of them, I threw a knot of money from my pocket for the little bit of work they had already done. It wasn't much, they were too busy frontin' for the hood. Guess they'd do anything but work for the clout.

"Skinny, call me when y'all get everything to the trucks. Y'all good? Or you need me to stay?"

"Man, I wish a nigga would," Skinny chuckled.

He barely weighed 120 pounds, but that was one deadly ass nigga, and everyone knew it. Walking to the back, I peeked in the bedroom, the boxes were stacked damn near to the top, which means the only one broken down was the room in the living room. Another crew would have to put in overtime tonight. It's cool, they'd eat double too. I'd make sure of that.

"Aye, I'm up."

Cranky because I was late for lunch with my wifey, I sped down the highway blasting Tupac. Hopefully, she understood. I had been working so hard to get her back I didn't want to fuck up what we were becoming. Chantel had no idea, but I was determined to make her my wife by the end of the year. Once I reached my house, I sat in the driveway reverting to Jared from J-Black for a few minutes. J-Black became my nickname because people said when I got angry, I blacked the fuck out. Entering my house from the side door, I stopped to get naked in the mudroom, calling Chantel to tell her I was home but in the burn room. She knew exactly what that meant. She said Chef Lance had left, so it was only us in the house.

"Hurry up," she added dryly.

Promising her I'd be out soon, we hung up.

Chapter Fifteen

GIANNA

Mr. Roberts

A week had passed since Two Sweets had been vandalized. The new tables were due in today, I decided to change the whole look of the seating to steel instead of wood. I was in the shop before sunrise, blending my special herbs of tea. The solitude of the morning put me in a zone that I knew would be hard for me to come out of. Mornings like this was when I created unheard of combinations that most were scared to even put in the same sentence. Music blaring throughout the speaker system, I hummed along with the melody playing from my playlist on Tidal.

My phone vibrated in my smock pocket, startling me. Surveying the sky to see if the sun was even up, I plucked the phone from my pocket with attitude. The calls, texts and harassment were beginning to wear on me. Between Alana and Sydney, I didn't know which one was worse. Both were sending messages from fake numbers, trying to convince me that their man loved them more. I tried my best to ignore them both, but things were growing out of control. On top of that, my parents believed I should go back to my husband like the good little wife they raised me to be. Little did they know, for the first time in my life, I was developing a true sense of who I was. I'm not as timid as I believed.

My eyes quickly scanned the text to see what bullshit that was being sent this morning. Pleasantly surprised to see that the message came from Noah, and he wanted to check in with me before starting his day. Noah and I had become closer than expected in a short period of time. The way everything happened was wild as hell, but my gut said it was fate. It didn't hurt that Noah was very easy on the eyes. Truth be told, the man was fine. Clench my thighs together, fine. Extra switch in hips, fine. Pretty dress, soft perfume, make sure my pedicure ain't chipped, fine. Noah was commit adultery, fine. His lopsided grin always reached his eyes, his vibe so sincere it made me wonder what the hell Alana was even thinking about getting caught out there. I knew he had cancer, and things had probably changed drastically in the bedroom, but damn.

My fingers grazed across the phone, returning his message. Engrossed in our conversation, I took a breather from mixing my herbs for the tea. Perching myself up on the counter, my feet were swinging banging against the cabinet doors below me. Noah was a riot even this early in the morning, I giggled through the whole conversation. I prayed our child had his personality. Unconsciously, I sighed, rubbing my flat stomach.

William messed up; my mind not even able to fully grasp where we went wrong. Perfect is not how I'd describe myself or anyone else, but I could honestly say I gave it my all.

My mother's sunrise devotional text cut through my thoughts. While everything was changing around me, I could always count on my mother's sunrise devotionals to remain a constant. Ever since I told my parents that I went through with being a parent without William, every morning text was a bible verse about marriage. Did they send William these messages? Most likely not, that double standard stuff made my blood boil. I'm sure he was still getting text messages about leadership and protection. Who prayed for my protection from William and his lies? His girlfriend? His disrespect of our union? No one. Not even my sexist parents. They wanted a perfect daughter to show off to the world but didn't cover my heart against that same world.

A sudden banging on the glass in the front of the bakery, had me leaping off the counter. Flexing my muscles in anticipation, I snatched the aluminum bat from the closet, now glad I made the purchase last week. I guess I'd find out which one of the desperate chicks, tore up my store today. Pissed, I rushed to the front of the store, only to find Noah standing there looking delicious in his tailored black suit. From the outside, he held up two canisters and a plain brown bag. Shaking my head, I unlocked the door holding it open for him to slide by me.

"What are you doing here, Noah?" I asked, lightly touching his arm.

"Once I knew you were up, I wanted to catch the sunrise with you, but I started getting caught up in our conversation and lost track of time. I know you have your own special blend of coffee, so I was kinda hoping you'd make us some, and we could sit and talk. And Lance, my brother's chef, made some breakfast sandwiches this morning. Jared has had him at the house for the last week," he answered, offering me the bag.

"Thank you for sharing, his food is hands down the best I've ever sampled. Why are you heading out this early if your meeting isn't until 8?"

"On meeting days, I always go in early, I like to personally make sure all my ducks are in a row."

"I understand that. I'm one of those people that find it hard to trust someone else will put as much love and care into my business as I do."

"Exactly, I didn't come this far to place my future in someone else's hands."

"Let me make us that tea, I was working on a new blend. You can be the first to try it with me," I offered.

"I'll try anything you want to serve me, Gia. Anything," he stated, sliding his arm around my waist, pulling me to him.

Gulping hard, my body melted into his strong arms, my nose filled with the smell of the Burberry Touch he had on. The last thing I wanted was to confuse our roles with the baby coming, my marriage on the fritz, being harassed by two different women, this was all too much for me. Slowly spinning in his arms to get him to release his hold, we were now face to face. My pulse quickened, the blood rapidly coursing through my veins. Lightheadedness took over my body. My knees gave in, causing me to falter a little. His strong arms caught me before I could actually fall, I just stumbled back some. Holding me close with his head buried in my neck, he asked if I was ok. The way his lips grazed my neck, had my eyes closing involuntarily.

"You okay, beautiful?" he mumbled.

"Yes, I just got a little dizzy. Haven't had much sleep lately," I confessed.

"I'd love to give you mouth to mouth, gorgeous but not under these conditions," he flirted.

"Are you flirting with me, Mr. Roberts? I'm a married woman, still," I confirmed halfheartedly.

"I say this with all due respect, fuck your husband, Ma."

Heat rose from the bottom of my feet to the follicles of hair on my head. This man literally just gave me a fever. A loud bang caused us to both jump swinging around to see where the commotion came from. Stunned that my parents were at the door, I saw what hit the glass. My mother was smacking the window with her bible. As old and tattered as it was, I'm shocked it didn't fall apart.

"Here we go," I uttered, pulling away from Noah.

"You don't have to face them alone," he whispered, yanking me back to him.

My mother started beating on the door even harder, while my father began calling and casting out demons in tongues. They were so extra at times. Asking Noah to set up the tea brewer with hot water, I jogged to the door to let my parents in, I knew the backlash of what they think they witnessed or were about to witness was going to be over the top. I've never been able to venture far from the life they wanted for me. Even in high school, my nickname was Perfect G because I always did things the right way. Broke no rules, was never late, never missed a day, my appearance was always neatly put together, I stayed inside the lines that my parents drew around my life.

"Good morning, mother, father," I greeted tensely.

"What in the hell is going on in here?" my father demanded.

"Noah came to bring me breakfast to start my day. I haven't been getting enough sleep or eating correctly, and I almost passed out. He caught me," I explained.

"Oh, dear. I know this isn't what you want to hear, but if you just went home to your husband who loves you, life would fall back into place seamlessly. William is sorry, honey, and he is willing to take you back, even with you being pregnant with someone else's baby," she whispered the last part the whole time her eyes glued to Noah.

"Oh, how nice of him," I snorted sarcastically.

"Good morning, Mr. and Mrs. Baxter. You're out early. I guess you also believe in the early bird gets the worm," he called the last part over his shoulder, turning his attention back to the tea brewer.

"Excuse me. Gia, can you come help me with this? I'm going to burn myself or the bakery down," Noah chuckled.

My father scoffed; he didn't want me around Noah. Even the pastor in him wouldn't allow him to acknowledge his greeting. My mother grunted a good morning, but my father just stared at him. Tension filled the air, I eased over to Noah to show him how to work the brewer. Advising that I needed to go get the tea, I slipped out the room. Scared to leave my parents in the room alone with Noah, I hurried about to get what I needed.

"Mom, dad, you never told me why you are here. And this early in the morning. Is something wrong?"

"We have business to take care of this morning. We had no intention of coming out this early, but when you didn't respond to your mother's sunrise devotion, we didn't know what to think. So, we came to check on you."

"Yes, darling, we worry about you being out here alone. Especially after the incident that happened. William checks on you every day through us; it's time you speak to him," my mother said, touching my face with the back of her hand.

"William slept in every morning while I prepared him breakfast and then came to the bakery to get started on my day. Which means this is nothing new for me. I am fine."

"Gia, I have to get going, but don't forget to eat your food. Thanks for the tea, I'll text you later," Noah stated.

"Her name is Gianna," my father stressed.

"Gia is just fine," I announced, rolling my eyes.

"Have a great day, Mr. and Mrs. Baxter," Noah grinned.

Kissing me on the cheek, he strolled out the door like he was on top of the world.

"Don't get too comfortable around him, Gianna. I'm telling you now that William is only going to put up with so much," my father urged.

"William? Is William your son? Or am I your daughter? I need to know because right now, I am confused. Why are you more concerned about his feelings than mine? Not once have you said anything about him cheating. Not once when I've come to either of you, have you given me any advice besides submit. Not once have you considered how this was making me feel. His slutty ass girlfriend came to my job, embarrassed me in front of my employees. Kissed bloody spit into my husband's mouth, she's harassing me day and night. She sent me videos of them having sex!" I screamed.

"Language, young lady!" my father shouted, banging his hand down on the counter.

"Is that all you have to say? Out of everything I just said? You want me to watch my language?" I huffed.

"Richard, let me talk to her," my mother suggested.

"Men sometimes go through a phase, baby. He will be back home, he knows that he cannot parade around town with that trollop," my mom said dismissively.

"I love both of you, but I need to start baking, so it's best if you left now."

Without another word, I showed them the door. I never wanted to be disrespectful to my parents, but my patience was wearing thin.

Chapter Sixteen

NOAH

The Businessman

"Our guests have arrived, Mr. Roberts. Meeting room two is all set-up and ready to go," my assistant Keisha confirmed.

"Thanks, Keish. Here I come, tell them I'm on a call, and I'll be right with them. Offer them water and coffee. You know what to do," I delivered.

"You need to make an entrance for this one?"

"If you only knew."

"I'll make it look good, boss. I got you covered."

Five minutes later, I entered the room to small chatter around the twelve-person table. Only six of custom ergonomic office chairs were occupied this morning. Keisha set out breakfast croissants in the middle of the table along with the water and coffee. Marching to the front of the room, I cleared my throat, gaining everyone's attention.

"Good morning, sorry for the delay. I had to take a call from my foreman that is currently on-site breaking ground this morning," I apologized.

"Oh, good morning again, Pastor and Mrs. Baxter," I greeted with a sly smirk.

Clapping my hands twice, I suggested we get down to business. Mr. Baxter's forehead was slick with sweat, Mrs. Baxter's eyes were still budging out of her head. Obviously, they weren't expecting me to be the owner of the construction company they were meeting with today. Doing my full research on what they were looking for, I knew that I was the last company in the area that they were meeting with. The others had blatantly refused to work with their budget. I also knew that my prices were normally slightly higher than the others. My work was immaculate, I created visions of greatness out of the best parts of my mind. Knowing my worth, I always went for the top dollar. Even though my everyday look didn't show it, I was easily a multi-millionaire.

"Does anyone have any questions?" I finished the presentation.

All eyes were planted on me, while I examined the look on everyone's face. One of their lawyers spoke first, asking a few legal questions. While he was going over a couple of things he had written down, Keisha came in the room with more coffee and now pastries from Two Sweets. Not missing the raised eyebrow from the Baxter's when the pastries were introduced to the table, I confirmed that I paid for them with a chuckle.

Mr. Baxter's shoulders were so high near his ears, I wanted

to laugh. This morning he was the one calling the shots; he couldn't even open his righteous mouth to speak when I greeted him. It's always the church people that pass judgment swearing that they are better than the people around them. Holier than thou. After doing my research, I figured out that Harmony Baptist Church was owned by Pastor and Mrs. Baxter. I planned to offer them the family discount. Technically, we're now family, given that Gianna was carrying my seed. But since he gave me his ass to kiss, fuck him and his weird looking wife.

"I prepared a folder for each of you to review and get back to us. Hope to hear from you soon," I said, politely dismissing them. Allowing Keisha to start clearing the table, I walked them to the elevators myself.

"Mr. Roberts, ummm, Noah, I had no clue this was your company. Wow. This," he spoke slowly, surveying the office with his arms stretched wide.

"This is amazing," he continued.

"Thank you, I will have a legacy to leave to my child," I added.

"Mr. Roberts, you have a call on line one," Keisha called from the bottom of the hall.

"Thank you, here I come," I called back.

"Have a great day," I spoke again, quickly shaking everyone's hands.

The light on my desk phone blinked rapidly, showing that I had a call holding on line one. Swiftly, I cross the room to grab the call off hold.

"This is Noah," I answered.

"No, it's me," Alana's voice trailed off.

"What's up, Lana?"

"You haven't paid the bills, and we're running low on food."

"Alana, I transferred the condo into your name, so you'd never be homeless. But we aren't out of food, you are. The bills are now your responsibility. Tell your man to pay them."

"You are my man, Noah. I don't want anyone else."

"That isn't what you said while you were out cheating. You even let that nigga beat raw," I hissed.

"I made a mistake! I got rid of mine; you still have a baby on the way with a total stranger. The whole family is celebrating a baby that should belong to me and you. How do you think that makes me feel? I'm trying here, No," she whined.

"Alana, I'm going to do you a solid. I'll pay the bills and put enough money in your account for food for the next year while you look for a job. After that, you're on your own, sweetie. And I'll be transferring the bills out of my name when the year is up. This will come with some rules for you to follow," I huffed, hanging up the phone.

Alana proved to be a thorn in my side at each step of me pulling away from her. She didn't think I knew she was calling Gianna all day and night, not only at the bakery but on her cell phone. I decided to draw up a legal contract to have her sign if she wanted to have me pay the bills in the house that I was no longer living in. Emailing my lawyer, I let him know what I needed, asking him to draw the paperwork up as soon as possible. Preferably by the end of the day. Placing a few calls to get some business done, I headed to my car to get the rest of my day started. My next stop, the new venture we were breaking ground on this morning. Turning up my music, I rode out to the other side of town to check in with my crew. I knew they'd clown me for being in a suit and tie today, but it was all good.

They were all happy with the pay they received and steady jobs, so when they saw me in a suit, they knew most likely I had secured the next location of work. My phone was still on vibrate, but the car picked up the call, cutting through the song that was playing. Checking the dashboard to see who was calling, I smiled to see it was my little boo, Gianna.

"Hey," I answered.

"Hey, yourself. Why didn't you tell me the meeting was with my parents?" she questioned.

"Honestly, I wanted it to be a surprise. I planned to offer them the family discount, but your father couldn't even return a simple hello this morning."

I shrugged like she could see me.

"I'm sorry about that. He almost never acts that way. But I respect it, it's your business and I understand how you feel. Oh well. By the way, that was the best breakfast sandwich I've ever had. What does Chef Lance cook with?"

"I don't know! It's like love in every bite," I chuckled.

"Are you busy tonight? If you are, I understand. If you aren't, do you mind coming by to keep me company for a while? I'll cook, but don't expect greatness. I haven't told my parents where I live yet because I know they will tell William. So, it's been pretty lonely. We can go over baby names and such."

"You said the magic word…food. I'll be there with bells on, but if your food is nasty, let's just order out for now and get you cooking lessons because I can't have you feeding our baby beans and franks forever."

"Boy, shut up. I'll text you this evening. My morning crowd is starting to gather in. Is 6 p.m. good?"

"Yes, I'll be there."

Three lights away from the destination, my lawyer called to let me know he had the paperwork ready for me to pick-up from the front desk at his office. Thanking him, I sped up to the construction site to see how my guys were doing.

The sun came blazing down on me as soon as I stepped out of the car, today was going to a be scorcher. Quickly, I retreated to the car to place my suit jacket in the car. With a quick roll up of my sleeves, I was on the move again. Sliding my Cartier aviator shades on my face, I picked up my pace speaking to everyone I could before reaching my foreman. By the time I left, it was break time, so I gave permission for lunch on me using the corporate card. My guys were happy as hell.

On my way to the lawyer's office to get the paperwork for Alana to sign, I texted my parents in a group message to just check on them. My mother responded first, telling me that I better stop by to see her soon. My father was working as always, so I didn't expect him to respond until much later.

When I reached the desk of the secretary, she handed me the folder with my request in it. The ease of the transaction reminded me why I choose this overpriced lawyer. You get what you pay for, and he was fast and efficient. We've never came across an issue he wasn't able to fix legally.

My chest constricted with anger as I approached my condo. Well, Alana's condo. I stood on the other side ringing the doorbell instead of using my key. Using my key would send mixed signals, which was something I didn't want to do. Alana came to the door smelling sweet like honey, looking sexy as hell in her wife beater and boy shorts. She knew damn well, I got weak every time I saw her like this. Shit. Why was she making this so hard?

"Why didn't you use your key?"

"I don't live here anymore."

"It's our home, no matter whose name is on the deed. Come on, No. You know that."

Stroking my beard, I just shot her a pointed look without acknowledging her statement. At one point in our relationship, my heart was so connected to hers; it was no way I'd leave her. For anything. In my mind, there wasn't nothing that could tear us apart. When I found out I had cancer, my outlook on life changed. Almost overnight, I knew what type of man I wanted to become. Alana and I sat down and discussed what was next. I followed through on my end, but apparently, she had no intention on staying true to her word. Part of me understood that we're still young, and it wasn't, but a year ago, we were both out there doing fuck shit. But the other part of me felt betrayed, my heart hurt for what I thought we had. Shit, Alana still stayed out half the night with her ratchet ass friends. She slept until at least noon, not even trying to put her degree to use. Her mother still struggled to pay her student loans.

"What terms do I need to agree to?" she asked with a smirk one hand on her hip.

At that moment, I knew that in her mind thinking I was going to be on some bullshit. The joke was on her, she wasn't going to like what I had drawn up. This was more about giving her a chance to get her shit together and protecting Gianna. It was imperative to me that Gia was at peace. Currently, Gianna and my seed were my top priorities.

"First, you will need to start looking for a job. Second, the most important thing is that you stop calling, texting, showing up at Gianna's bakery. Stop sending your raggedy ass friend there too," I firmly spoke.

"Noah, I don't be messing—"

I cut her off from finishing her lie. My palm raised in a stop motion.

"Aht, aht. It's done. My job is to make sure my seed is not stressed, which means she cannot be stressed. If you think calling her from different numbers, blocked numbers, sending anyone up there is going to fly...it won't. Try me," I threatened.

"But baby, you act like we don't belong together. I just want her out the way. We can co-parent with her. However, she doesn't deserve this unlimited access to you. Let her husband worry about her," she cried.

Not moved by her tears, I pointed out the highlighted parts of the contract. Stomping her feet like a damn two-year-old, she snatched the papers out of my hand, flinging herself on the couch. Huffing and puffing, she sat there with her chest rising and falling hard. I parked myself on the couch in front of her giving her the unphased face. Once I got tired of waiting out her tantrum, I asked her if she was going to read and sign the papers or if I should go.

"I can't believe you'd really stoop this low, Noah. You promised to always take care of me," she whined.

"While you were mine, not while you belong to someone else. I'm a generous man, but I'm nobody's fucking fool. Either sign it or you don't doesn't make a difference to me. However, on me, you will leave Gianna the fuck alone. She hasn't done anything to you. Hell, the way you're carrying it, she may block me out of my child's life. That won't be good for you, if it comes to that," I warned.

"I'm going to sign the damn papers, Noah. Just let me read them first, damn."

"Thank you."

"Let me drop them off to your office tomorrow. I have an appointment in thirty minutes, and I want to read through it. I'll even have my signature notarized, so I can't pretend it wasn't me. Anything to make you see that I'm trying to do right," she smiled weakly.

"Okay, Alana, but if you aren't there with these papers signed tomorrow, the deal is off."

"I got it, Noah," she huffed.

Exiting the condo, all I could do was pray that she wasn't on no bullshit. Alana had always been a wildcard, but I'd choke her ass out if she kept fucking with Gianna.

Chapter Seventeen

CHANTEL

No Words

"Welcome back, Chantel!" my co-worker, Missy, greeted.

"Thank you. Good morning, ladies," I called out.

"Girl, we are so happy to have you back. It's been crazy. I hope everything is better with your family. I heard you were out due to a family emergency. And Pamela got fired a couple of days after you went out. Chile, it has been a circus up in here," Harriet, my older co-worker, spoke.

Giggling at Harriet's country accent, I got caught up on what else went on around the office while I was out. Harriet always had an earful for anyone that would listen. Before I had the chance to get settled in my seat good, my desk phone rang. My boss was beckoning me to come to his office. The hair on the back of my neck stood up. Nervous that he was still going to fire me, I slowly made my way to his office.

"Hey, Anthony. You needed to see me?"

"Yes, shut the door behind you."

"Umm, is everything okay?"

"Yes, I wanted to personally welcome you back. Also, give a gentle reminder that under no circumstances can we allow this type of thing to blow over again. I hope you've learned your lesson during your time off."

"I have. Thank you, it feels good to be back. You don't have to worry about anything like this happening again. I can promise you that," I smiled faintly.

"Okay, that is great to hear. We have a busy workload today. So, I'll let you get to it."

"Okay."

As I turned to leave the office, Anthony caught me off guard with his next words.

"Oh shoot, Chantel. Most importantly... Congratulations!" he chirped.

Confused, I flung myself back around to face him. What the fuck was that supposed to mean?

"Congratulations?"

"Yes, on your new addition to the family. I saw Alana when she came to sign for the vials. I'm surprised she didn't have them sent directly to an IVF center. Either way, it was good to see her in such good spirits despite everything that has transpired," he spelled out.

"Thank you," I stuttered.

Slipping the door shut behind me, once it closed, I leaned against it with my head back. My eyes snapped shut. Suddenly,

I had a headache. Rubbing my temples, my lips pressed into a straight line, I walked back to my desk to prepare for my first client of the day. With my mind made up to get through my day and deal with the Alana bullshit later, I focused on checking my emails to get caught up until my first client showed up.

The day breezed by faster and smoother than any day I've ever had at work. Queasiness seized my stomach, my body quivered with panic. I would rather bury my head in the sand than tell Noah that Alana signed out a vial of his sperm for herself. Shit. Maybe she just wanted to scare him into believing she had the upper hand so that he'd be at her mercy. Lord knows that girl wasn't mentally nor emotionally ready to be anyone's mother. She refused to take responsibility for herself, what the hell would she do with a baby?

Powering my phone back on, a million messages popped up from my mother, Noah, Jared, and Alana. Based on the conversations, the cat was already out the bag. I released a breath that I didn't realize I was holding. Alana's messy ass sent a group text picture of an empty vial next to the paperwork of Noah's storage. When they broke up, none of us even thought to remove her name from the authorized people to release his sperm to. My mind was spinning, thinking about how Noah felt in this moment. One baby on the way from a complete stranger and possibly a baby on the way by someone he used to love but now loathed. Damn. Instead of responding, I just headed straight to Jared's. This bitch was going to cause me to drink.

"Hey, baby," I announced, opening the front door.

"Hey, Ma. What the fuck is wrong with your ditzy ass sister?" Jared attacked as soon as I entered the space.

"I'm not my sister, Jared. Can you please greet me before you jump down my damn throat?" I scoffed.

"Sorry, baby. You're right. You've never been like her, which is why I love you," he apologized between kisses.

My attitude eased with each kiss his lips delivered. Butterflies swarmed my stomach, just being in his presence caused me to be giddy. This man was too irresistible. No matter how hard I tried to convince myself and everyone around us that he did not affect me that, shit was a lie. A boldface lie. His lips tasted like caramel, I sucked them into my mouth. Moaning as my insides heated up with each slippery kiss. The way we had been going at it lately had been so intense that I wasn't sure how much longer I could be celibate. Shit, I wanted to give his ass the business today. Tomorrow. Every day. If it was up to me, I'd eat, sleep and breathe this delectable man.

My hands caressed his baby smooth skin on his face. Looking deep into his eyes, my heart pounded with love for him that I was still too scared to express. After I stole another short kiss, I pushed away from him, making my way to the bar to get a drink. I needed something strong, opting for Grey Goose and cranberry juice, my go-to drink. Drink in hand, I sat Indian style on the couch across from Jared. We talked about my first day back to work, while I slowly sipped my concoction. At some point, the buzz of my drink overcame me. I found my way to his lap, straddling him, smothering him with wet kisses from his lips to his neck.

"Baby, you have to stop. It's only so much I can handle before I slide into them guts," he warned.

"Maybe that's what I want," I said suggestively.

His hand slid up my shirt, twirling my nipple between his thumb and pointer finger. My breath hitched; the groan stuck in the back of my throat.

"Jared," I panted.

"Yes, baby," he hummed.

His manhood so hard I just knew it was strong enough to break through my nursing scrubs. Not wanting to waste any more time, I raised my shirt over my head, promptly unhooking my bra. My titties bounced out happy to be freed. My nipples were enlarged with lust waiting to be sucked.

"Shit," Jared croaked out.

"Suck them please, baby," I pleaded.

Obliging, Jared immediately pushed both breasts together, sucking them hard into his mouth.

"Yes," I shouted, throwing my head back.

"Bae, get up."

"We taking this to the room?"

"Nah, man. We can't do this right now," he answered, swiping a hand down his face.

Angry, I hopped up from his lap. How dare he deny me? Was this all a game to him, was he on some get back type shit? I know I wasn't ready to give it up before, but at this moment, I was ready to offer him my pussy on a platter. The nerve of this nigga. Fuck he look like telling me no? Scrambling to fix my bra, I grabbed my shirt off the floor. It was time to go, I was moving around so fast I felt the squishiness of my lovebox, dampening my thighs.

"Chantel, it's not what you're probably thinking. I want you more than anything, I can promise that. Look at this dick, your dick, that's so hard for you right now it hurts," he persisted.

"Why do I want to look at some dick you don't want to share?" I shouted.

He had me all in my feelings. See, this is why I've remained single and celibate all this time. Niggas played too many damn games for me. All of a sudden, I felt like the house was smothering me, I needed to get the hell out of here.

"Chan, you made the decision to be celibate years ago. I wasn't man enough to respect your decision then. This time I want to show you that I'm your forever. You will be my wife. Let me ride this out with you," he explained.

Shit. This is exactly what I wanted to hear a couple of years back, but instead, he skated. For the second time tonight, my anger dissipated almost as easily as it came. Gone. Vanished. Non-existent.

'What if I'm ready now?"

"Nah. Until you become Mrs. Roberts, you aren't ready."

"When will I be Mrs. Roberts, Mr. Roberts?" I asked sassily.

"We can get married tomorrow if you like. Check the laws and requirements."

He said it so matter of fact that it sent chills down my back. A smile eased across my face. Rolling my eyes to the ceiling, I pushed him in disbelief.

"Boy, I bet if I called you tomorrow on my lunch break saying meet me at the courthouse, you'd be singing a different tune."

"Tomorrow is a little too quick. You want to elope without our family?"

"Of course not, Jared. All I'm saying is, you're just talking because you have lips."

"Talking because I have lips, huh?"

"Yeah, that's what I said."

"Welp, guess the only thing left to do is prove it to you. I'm not letting you go this time, Ms. Mann. It's not even an option. I'm not interested in no consolation prize in this game of love. Shorty, I want you. The one number, my one and only. That shit is facts. I've omitted some dumb shit before, but I ain't never lied to you. Ya boy too through for that shit, I'm about my word. You know that much. You just don't understand how much I'm in love with you."

Too overwhelmed to speak, I simply nodded, leaving him standing in the middle of the living room. As I walked into the kitchen, I heard keys jingling at the door. Noah came into the house. His face showed defeat all over it. He walked in, head hanging down, his shoulders hunched over as if he was carrying the weight of the world on them.

"Hey, No," I spoke.

"Chan," he acknowledged.

"Hard day?"

"Hard ain't the word, sis."

The day that he found out he had cancer, he didn't look this worn. My poor bestie had been getting beat up in life recently. Alana wasn't shit for the stunt she pulled. I was sure that if there was a point where he may have taken her back, that shit was dead now. She had always been known to take things too far, then play the victim. It had been plenty of times I asked my mother if she was really her child. Her behavior was so different from the person my mother tried to raise; it was baffling to me. We had the same mother and father. My father passed away a little after my mother had me, so I had no recollection of him. All I knew was the stories my mother and grandparents told me about him.

"Go take a shower, I'll cook you up some food and make you a strong drink," I offered.

"Thanks, bestie. I just want to relax, so that sounds great. I don't even want to talk about this shit. It's nothing I can do about it; she's already used it. I'm going to have two babies at once, like some ghetto ass nigga. The only problem is I ain't get no pussy from either of them to make this happen," he sighed.

"Shit's crazy, but if anyone can get through it, it's you. Plus, you have us. Once Alana drops that baby, I'm putting my hands on her. First, she tried to get me fired, and now this? Nah, she needs to catch these hands. Now, it makes perfect sense on why she snitched. Ain't no way I would've let her take that sperm out of there. She needed to get me out the way for her plan to work. Ole funky conniving ass," I grimaced.

"Man, we will love the baby when it gets here. I hope it's a boy and a girl that way your funky ass sperm don't have to be spread around like butter no more. You can destroy whatever is left. This shit is the true definition of being trapped into fatherhood. We can't even yell at you for not strapping up. You ain't even been diving in the ocean. That has to be the most tragic part of all of this. Is your dick working again, little man?" Jared laughed, always making a joke out of something.

"Ain't shit about me little, nigga. And at this point, it doesn't matter. I think after this shit, it may never get up again out of fear of more drama," Noah answered, throwing his arms in the air before walking off towards his room.

Chapter Eighteen

5 MONTHS LATER

Jared

Best of Both Worlds

The night of the Mayor's Ball was rapidly approaching. The excitement was heavy amongst my family. Not only because of the chance of meeting the president, but they knew what else I had up my sleeve. The Tiffany Soleste cushion-cut yellow diamond, I was eyeballing from Tiffany's, was created for Chantel's ring finger. Chantel would soon be my wife. My days as a single man were almost over. The shallow part of me wanted to call up all my old bitches for one last night of sin. I'd have to tag-team them though, I used to have so many hoes. The sensible part of me reminded myself that not only would Chantel kill me, but my family would help her hide the body. My brother, my parents, and just about everyone in my family was smitten with

Chantel. It was easy to see why. She was beautiful, bubbly, ingenious, respectable, and loyal as hell.

Excitedly, I tapped the laptop keys, hitting the submit button. Done. I purchased the ring for Chantel, my heart thudding with different emotions. When I walked away from Chantel the first time, in my mind, it was forever. But my heart kept circling back to her. No matter how I tried to block her out, the heart wants what the heart wants. I made the right decision to walk away at the time because I wasn't ready to settle down. Now, if the very thought of her not being in my life crept in my mind, I'd lose it.

Slouching back in the chair I was sitting in, I closed my eyes, picturing the way I hope Chantel would react. I couldn't figure out if I wanted her to cry standing there with a stuck look plastered on her face, or if I'd be more flattered for her to jump in my arms screaming

"YES." Either way, all I knew was the answer better had been yes. Anything other than the correct answer, and I'd rock bottom the hell out of her. Never had I put my hands on a woman or even thought it was ok to, but the wrong answer would be bad for her health. All this free pussy I was giving up for her, I still had women blowing up my phone whining about how much they missed me. The truth was, I wasn't thinking about none of them hoes.

"Jared, I'm out for the day, bruh. You enjoy your weekend," Chef Lance informed.

"A'ight, bruh. I'll get up with you soon. Thanks for coming through early this week," I responded.

Chef Lance was a bulky brother that just looked like he could make anything taste good. I wouldn't go as far as to say he was fat, but the potbelly on him said he tasted everything he's ever made. Short in stature, his frame didn't give away his strength. I've seen him throw, pick up a nigga, and fling him across the room like he was tossing a football to his son. We grew up together around the way. My parents still live down the street from his. When he got locked up for identity theft, I checked in on him a few times. While in the joint, he discovered a love for cooking from working in the jailhouse kitchen. Since he went to jail for some white-collar scam shit, life wasn't too hard to jump back into when he got out. Promising his parents he'd stay out of trouble, he enrolled in culinary arts school. When he was attending school, I'd hire him to cook for me and different family events. Sometimes a person just needed a support system that believed in them to make the right change for their life.

Double-checking the time, I got up to head out to the Mayor's office again. Tired of meeting up with this cheesy ass, always up to something fool, I was going to let him know that I wasn't on his payroll to be at his beck and call. This shit was for the birds. I knew for sure he never called the others the way he called me. Maybe he didn't think my gangster was strong enough to tell him to kiss my ass. Whatever it was that he needed or requested today, better be the last thing. Or he might find himself six feet under. This blackmail thing was becoming a thorn in my side. The only good thing from all of this was that I felt like I was rebuilding the communities closest to me instead of tearing them down.

The drugs were still in the areas I moved out of, but it was nowhere near as rampant as before. I moved weight like a legend, an OG, a God. Pills, coke, crack, heroin, weed, meth, I sold it all. It didn't matter what it was, I could sell money to the US Treasury, weave to a show pony, shit water to a well. My gift of gab had gotten me far in my life. The difference between me and the rest of these niggas was, my word was bond. I treated my word golden. If I said it, I meant that shit. Wasn't no two ways about it. What is a man without his word? My daddy taught us that. We lived it, breathed it, believed in it.

Donning my NY Yankees fitted cap halfway on my head, I stepped into my Timb's on my way out the door to the appointment with the Mayor. The beat from the music I was blasting shook the whole car. It was almost like I could feel the words course through my body. The pre-rolled blunt was staring at my ass from the ashtray, I licked my lips but decided to wait until I finished up the meeting with William. Not having a clue what he wanted this time, I may need to spark one once I got back to the car. I hoped the twisted lip receptionist was at lunch when I got there because I didn't have the patience for her snotty attitude today. Soon as I entered the building, the receptionist and I locked eyes. Running my hand down my face I tried to hide my displeasure. Surprisingly, she smiled in my direction. Was she taunting me?

"Hi, Mr. Roberts. Mayor Wesley should be out to get you soon. His meeting before yours ran over, they are discussing the next fiscal quarter," she spoke.

She gave away too much information that I didn't give a fuck about with a faint smile tugging at her lips. Most of the time, her ass would barely lift her eyes to meet mine when I came in. Why was she so friendly today?

"Umm, thank you. I'll just take a seat over here," I said.

"Can I ask you a question?" she hesitantly whispered.

"What's up?" I questioned cautiously, not sure where this was going.

"Do you really own three rehab centers across the state?"

"I do."

"This is embarrassing, but do you think you could give me a flyer or brochure? Any type of information that I could read up on? My daughter is struggling with an addiction that she can't seem to get a grip on," she uttered, leaning forward to keep the conversation quiet. My eyebrow raised in wonder, almost not believing the complete turn of events. Miss High and Mighty needed something from me.

"I'm sorry to hear that. Yes, I have some flyers in the car. I'll go grab you one now, we'd love to help her get back to the respectable young lady you know and love," I responded, putting my rehab pitch voice on.

"Thank you. You know I don't mean this in a disrespectful way, but I remember when drug addictions were a black problem. Only the riffraff or the people in the hoods were doing drugs. It's so mainstream now that we have to wake up and see what's going on around us. It's reached the suburbs and well just everywhere. I love Mayor Wesley's approach and attempt to get everyone the help that they need. I didn't know that's what your monthly meetings were about until I researched your name. I love the work you boys are doing on the "Teens Back Home" initiative program," she went on.

"Us what?" I inquired, my forehead wrinkled at the blatant disrespect.

"Boys. Well, I mean men, but you get what I'm saying. Don't take it out of context, please. I always address people as boys or girls," she stammered.

"People or black people?"

"You... gentlemen, I did not mean any disrespect. I was just trying to give a compliment," she huffed.

The same nerve I hit in her, she had hit in me. I refused to back down to her or to anyone with her way of thinking. Why did it always seem that when certain people so-called complimented you, it was backhanded as hell? The hallway filled with noise and people, it looked like his meeting was finally over. Wanting to drop a little knowledge on her, before I moved away from the desk, I left her with a jewel to ponder on.

"By the way, the government dropped those very drugs in our "hoods" breaking up families, destroying lives and making us weak for something that was killing us from the inside out. It was systematic the way most of these things are for the uhh, what you call us? The riffraff. The issue is it only became a problem when it hit the suburbs because that was never the plan. It was meant to overtake us completely, but like everything else, in the world, we found a way to beat it. Without all the extra help, the suburbs and white people get it. Only now it became a problem because it's not only affecting people of color," I scoffed, turning on my heels.

She sat there with her face beet red, so visibly upset, she was shaking. It always made me feel good to put her type in their place. Nothing about me was racist, but what I wouldn't do was give a racist a pass. Ever. That shit just wasn't happening.

"Are you okay?" one of the men coming down the hallway rushed over to her.

"Yeah, she's good. We were just having a conversation about her daughter being a drug addict and how she didn't think it could or should affect her or her family because she doesn't live in the hood like black people," I spoke loud enough for everyone around me to hear.

William shook his head while everyone else had their eyes trained on her to see if I was telling the truth. She broke down crying, probably of embarrassment more than anything, but I didn't give a damn. Fuck these old, I'm so much better than you broads that had more secrets in their closest than a little bit.

"Good afternoon, Mayor Wesley. Are you available now? I'm on a tight schedule today," I exaggerated, tapping the glass screen on my Rolex.

"Sure. I know you're a busy man with all the work you're

doing in the various communities, thank you for waiting," Mayor Wesley announced.

"Come on back," he said, motioning me towards his office with a sweep of his hand.

Securing the door behind us, I blew out a breath of frustration between my clenched lips.

"What's up, William? Why am I here today?"

"First, let me say I'm sorry for these racist ass people in here. I hate the dynamics of this shit. I don't hold meetings here with any of the others because they all have records of some sort. And these muthafuckas are noisy as hell. She actually googled you. Can you believe that shit? She needs to be worried about her meth head, rotten teeth, dirty, greasy head ass daughter," he argued.

"I'm not coming in here again. So, let's make this the last time before I get arrested for assault 'cause Karen out there gonna have me beat her ass all over this office," I threatened.

"Understood. I need you to take care of something for me. Or, if you can't, set up what I need. My home life is crazy right now, my wife has been cozying up to someone else. I'll admit I fucked up, but this nigga gotta go. I don't know who he is right yet, but I'll have the information to give you the night of the ball. Is that cool?" he quietly spoke.

"I won't make any promises, but let me think about it. We can talk about it more after you give me the information. Anyway, I have to go. I'm up," I replied, throwing up the peace sign on my way out the door.

Goosebumps traveled up the back of my neck. For some

reason, I bad feeling about what William was asking me to do. Nothing about me was afraid to kill, I just felt indifferent about the request. Why did he come to me? Was this a set-up to always have something to hold over my head? Not only that, I know this fool didn't think I was murdering some nigga his wife was fucking for free. Yes, I had murdered people previously, and I knew I'd have to pay for those sins, but I refused to add on to them without a price I could live with. If I decided to go through with this, he needed to know I was not doing anything outside of our current contract again. Shit, he said the rest of them fools already had records and shit. Why was he asking me to do his dirty work? Sparking my blunt as soon as I reached the car, I rode off in silence. My mind swirling around what my next move was going to be.

Chapter Nineteen

ALANA

Pay Attention to Me

Noah barely had two words for me these days like I wasn't the love of his life carrying his baby. Why did it matter how it happened? If he didn't want me to have access to his swimmers, he shouldn't have put my name on the paperwork. I'm just saying, we both knew we'd be back together at some point. I did what I did to make it happen sooner. Now, the whole family was looking at me funny as hell. Their opinions of me didn't matter. As long as I got Noah back, I'd be good if I never had to speak to them again. They could all kiss my ass. Each and every one them. Pretending that they'd never done something drastic to get the attention of the person they loved. Miss me with that bullshit. My momma always said young and dumb went together. Which meant at some point even his funky faced parents did some dumb shit, I wasn't sweating it anymore. At some point, when Noah and I were back together, they'd be back on my side.

My comfort was deeply rooted in the fact that once this baby got here, he'd see that we were meant to be. As soon as Noah came to his senses, I'd drop Rico like a bad habit. I was growing sick of his mooching ass. A man was supposed to be a provider and take care of his woman. Rico was barely taking care of himself after Jared's selfish ass cut him and his partners off. Rico was checking out a new connect but didn't have enough cash to cover the first package, so he and a few friends were going to pool their money together. Four grown ass men that had been hustling for years, and none of them had enough put aside to cop their weight from someone? Where they do that at? Either Jared was not being fair with them or these muthafuckas were slow and hustling backward.

"Ms. Mann?" the nurse called my name.

Noah stood up across from me when I stood. We faced off in silence. Sensing the tension boiling between us, she nervously rustled her papers with her head down.

"Umm, you can follow me. First, we will get your weight right over here to the left. You can place your stuff in the chair," she announced.

I tried to hand Noah my purse and jacket, but he nodded his head towards the empty chair. He was in full asshole mode today, I bet he held Miss thang's stuff. He probably held her hand, rubbed her feet, kissed her belly, and all types of first-time dad shit. Just the thought of that bitch made my skin crawl. Yes, we all know it was an accident on how she ended up with Noah's sperm, but damn, did she have to come in and take over? Here I was the loving girlfriend since high school, and she showed up taking my man from me. She didn't help him change the sheets after a cold sweat. She wasn't the one not being able to sleep because he was throwing up so loud in the bathroom. The cancer treatment took a toll on both of us. Like the doting girlfriend, I was there every step of the way. Well, almost. A girl still has to live her life too. I fucked up, but damn, it's been months. It's time to move on.

"Okay, everything looks great. We are in room 4 today. You can place your stuff in there now if you like, but I need you to do a urine sample for me, please," the nurse instructed.

Again, I passed my stuff to Noah, so my hands would be free. Reluctantly, he allowed me to give him my items. It wasn't much, but it was progress. I smiled on the inside.

"Thank you, I'll meet you in there after I use the bathroom," I said, trying to make small talk.

He followed the nurse to the room I was being seen in without a sound. Sometimes I hated how stubborn this damn boy could be. If he just saw things my way, we'd be happy and in love again. My feelings were hurt the nights I'd call him saying the baby and I were hungry, and instead of making a personal delivery to me, I'd get a cash app of fifty dollars saying get whatever I wanted to eat. Not that I didn't need or want the money, but he had no reason to be that cold towards me, the mother of his child. Tina and I had staked out his office plenty of times and found that most nights he made sure to take Gianna food. Or they'd go out together looking more like a couple than anything. Something had to give because at the end of the day, I was not losing my man to her or anyone else.

Finished in the bathroom, I scurried down the hall to the room. The bathroom was stinking from someone before me, and the smell of bad guts was stuck in my nose. Whoever used the bathroom before me needed to learn to at least wipe off the seat from their urine spraying everywhere. I hated that nasty shit, and from the looks of it, they didn't even wash their nasty hands. Even though the stench was fresh, the stink was dry, and the only paper towels in the trash were mine. A rap on the door cut me off from telling Noah about how dirty people were and my bathroom experience. If we were anywhere else, I'd be a little ticked off about our limited personal time being interrupted.

"Hello, good to see you both again," the doctor greeted.

"Hello, doc." Noah grinned for the first time I've laid eyes on him today.

"How are you feeling, Ms. Mann? Has the nausea calmed down yet?"

"Actually, it has! Finally, I just knew it would never end," I chuckled.

In my head, I wondered if I was so sick before I had just had an abortion right before getting pregnant again. I'd never question that out loud though, I didn't want anyone to judge me.

"Okay. let's get started, shall we?" she suggested.

A knot formed in my stomach when she wasn't able to

find the baby's heartbeat. Noah sat up with concern etched all over his face. He tried to blink the nervousness off his face, but it was too late, I caught it the moment I glanced over at him. He bit the side of his lip, then quickly stroked his beard, which was a sign that he was fearful. While I was terrified myself, parts of me warmed at the sight of him being nervous about the baby were created. It wasn't created the normal way, but it was out of love no matter what anyone thought.

A strong heartbeat came through the doppler, and we both instantly calmed down. Noah slid back in the chair from the edge he had moved down to. Hoping he wouldn't reject my hand, I reached behind me with my hand out, offering for him to take it in his. Pleasantly surprised, he took my hand, giving it a gentle squeeze. I knew in that moment I was going to get my man back. Everything up until this minute no longer mattered. It would be Noah Roberts and Alana Mann once again. Finally.

Since I had already pre-scheduled most of my appointments, I didn't need to stop at the front desk for anything. We strolled outside. Thanking Noah for showing up, I asked if I could call him later just to talk. He rebuffed, walking away from me without acknowledging my question, changing my whole mood. We just shared a moment of fright and relief in the doctor's office, and now he was back to acting like he didn't give a damn about me. If this was his childish way of breaking me down, it was working. I was growing tired of begging him to do the right thing. I've followed him, and the church mouse bitch enough around to know he didn't treat her this way.

Tina and I were working on getting a way to prove to everyone that she was not the goody two shoes everyone believed her to be, even if it was fabricated. My goal was to get my man back and possibly having him take custody of their child for us to raise as our own. She could just start over with the sperm she was supposed to get in the first place. If we found enough dirt on her, it'd be so much easier to get my man back. Our babies were not that far apart, only within months of each other. They'd almost be like twins; her baby the evil twin of course.

Maybe Noah would consider paying my mother to quit her job and help me around the house. I honestly didn't have a true motherly bone in my body. It was no way in hell I'd be content with just being home all day changing pampers and all that other shit. So, I knew he needed to have a plan in place. Hell, I did not make this baby by myself. Well, I did, but he was still the father. We also needed to talk about the contract he had in place, he needed to void that now since I was pregnant. Why would I look for a job now? He wasn't thinking straight.

Watching Noah pull out the parking lot without so much as a goodbye, I turned my attention to my ringing phone in my purse. I trampled in the direction of my car, getting in as I answered Rico's call. Rico was becoming more and more clingy. I wasn't sure if it was my pregnancy hormones or not, but I was just about over his broke ass.

"Bring that pregnant pussy to me, girl."

"Hello to you too, Rico. Yes, my appointment went well. Thank you for asking," I remarked.

"My bad, baby. How was the appointment? I just missed you, that's all. I haven't seen you in two days. You been hiding from daddy?"

"No, Rico. I've been busy trying to find a job," I lied.

"Yeah, well, come get me. I'm sick of this side of town for the night, I already packed a bag for your place."

"Okay, but you can only stay one night. My mom is coming to stay with me for two weeks, so I have to drop you back off tomorrow when I live the house," I lied again.

"Are you ashamed of me? Now I can't stay with my woman because your mom is there?" he questioned, his voice laced with anger.

"No, I'm not ashamed of you, babe. But my mom has been helping me pay the bills, and if you are here when she's here, she will stop helping me. Why would she help pay bills when I have an able-bodied man laid up in here with me?"

"That ain't my spot, that's yo' shit. I don't live there. So, why would I fork over money for a place I don't live in? That's some stupid shit, yo," he barked.

"My mom doesn't live here either. She has her own bills, including two of my student loans. So, really the thought isn't stupid," I barked back.

"Whatever, yo. Just come get me. You can bring me home tomorrow."

Chapter Twenty

GIANNA

My Salvation

y head tilted in the direction of my mother's voice. I knew damn well she didn't just say what I thought she said. My parents were coming so hard at my neck about going back home to William, I was over both of them. At this point, I was internally kicking myself for even agreeing to come visit them today. My father had begun a four-part sermon on forgiveness at church—his not so subtle way of reminding me that we are required to turn the other cheek. Hearing enough of his last sermon, I texted him to ask him to preach a four-part sermon on adultery. It was a part of the Ten Commandments, but you trying to tell me forgiveness is more important. Yeah, ok.

"Did you hear me, Gianna?" my mother coarsely whispered.

The hurt in her voice caught my attention again.

"I heard you. It's hard to believe that daddy cheated on you at the beginning of your marriage. I'm glad you were able to work through your issues. But I am not you, and William is not daddy. And we are not living in the same times," I spat.

"Darling, all relationships are tested. No one ever said marriage was easy. The bible says, "Therefore what God has joined together, let no one separate," she quoted.

"Mark 10:9," I replied dryly.

"Look, mom, I love you. I love dad. But I also love myself, this is it for me. I refuse to be disrespected. Given the outlandish way this woman showed up at my bakery, my place of business, says she separated us. Have you ever stopped to think that all marriages aren't put together by God? Yes, William is an awesome mayor. He's well educated, well-respected, and he wants the best for everyone in Ohio. But he is a lousy husband. He didn't support me starting my own business. He felt his dream was enough for the both of us as if I was no longer a person. We were supposed to be a team, not a one man show," I cried, breaking down as the stream of tears rolled down my face.

Stroking my hair gently away from my face, my mother lovingly dried my tears with the tip of her thumb. We no longer lived in the times where wives didn't have any other options. Divorce is more common than actually getting married these days. Most people just shacked up or jumped around from relationship to relationship. Situationships. Kids out of wedlock and not a single person tries to hide it. We were living in different times that haven't caught up to my parents. Back in the day, they had to hide any outside kids. Now, not a single soul would bat an eye at the circumstances. It seemed my parents were always the exception to every rule.

"My precious baby, William is trying to right his wrong. You need to at least hear him out. I know you can make your own decisions, but please just talk to the man. Seriously. He's been praying with your father day in and day out. Your father and I were happy to hear you agreed to at least show up to help him save face at the Mayor's Ball. He needs you, dear. He gets that now. He can't show up to his ball that the President of the United States will be attending without you on his arm. That would be the talk of the town. Plus, he is willing to help you co-parent with the young man Noah. He wants to set provisions in place, but he's willing to work this out. I'm so proud of his progressive way of thinking," she said.

It was so sad to me that so many older women still thought this way. While I didn't regret an ounce of my upbringing, I was finally coming into my own woman. No longer was I held by the shackles of the strict religious life my parents forced down my throat. My heart ached over the fact that they still saw William as the best thing since sliced bread. My broken heart didn't mean a thing to them as long as they saved face in the church and community.

"After this ball is over, I'm filing for divorce," I solemnly informed her.

"Baby, you will go to hell for divorcing him," she began to cry.

"I love you. But it's not up for discussion," I said, kissing her cheek.

The conversation was over, I listened to her pleading for months. Listened to my father's sermons, his begging for me to do the right thing by going back to William. Praying daily for healing and peace, my mind was made up, I was done. Leaving my mother with her head buried in her hands, I patted her back on the way out of the house. Those crocodile tears weren't going to eat away at my soul, today. Tuh.

Noah's key slid in the lock after a brief knock on the door. Since him, Chantel, and Jared were the only people that knew where I lived, I needed to make sure someone had a key. Plus, I wanted to make sure he had complete access to the baby when it came. We weren't in a relationship or anything, but the pull of attraction between us was undeniable. It was something I never felt before. Raw, uncharacteristic of everything I had ever been taught. Whenever we touched, even if it was accidental, it felt like an electric shock to my system.

"Gia, you decent?" he called before entering the apartment.

"Yes, come in," I answered.

Intensely, I observed his demeanor as he trotted through the door. His face always gave away his true feelings, no matter if it was good or bad. Without taking another step inside, he took off his construction boots, leaving them the front door. Leaving the boots on the mat, he advanced towards me, smiling.

"How was your day?"

I smiled.

"Good. Judging by how you look, I'd say you definitely worked harder than me today," I chuckled.

My eyes glazed over every inch of his appearance. Ninety-five percent of the time after work, he always looked so rugged. It amazed me how a man with a huge office in a beautiful building choose to stay in the field as much as possible. It was such a turn-on.

"Nothing like a hard day of work for a man to feel complete," he grinned.

Strangely enough, Noah and I fell into an agreeable routine over the last five months or so. Twice a week, he'd stay the night with me, to do anything extra I needed help with around the house and to just keep me company. He slept on the pull-out couch in the baby's room when he stayed. I'd cook dinner for us, we'd stay up watching movies, or playing games. Sometimes we'd just talk about our thoughts and ideas as we both worked on our leftover work from the day. Neither of us would have imagined this being the outcome of me being the accidental recipient of his sperm. This was not the future I saw in my dreams when I was laying on the table at the IVF office. But I had to admit this was so much better than anything I could dream up on my own.

"I'm going to take a quick shower, wash off some of this day. You need me to do anything beforehand?"

"Nope, you stink. Straight to the shower you go, sir!"

"I will rub your face in my sweaty armpit, kept getting smart," he teased.

"Oh no, I want no parts of that! Dinner should be ready by the time you get out since you take forever to primp like a girlllllllll," I taunted.

He fixed his lips like he wanted to say something but shook his head, keeping his thoughts to himself instead. He walked to the bathroom to get his hygiene together. Since the sun had long gone down, I wobbled over to the window to put down the blinds. A quick peek out the window caused me to do a double-take, I swore I saw Noah's ex-girlfriend across the street in a busted-up car. Clearly, I was seeing things, so I just closed the blinds tight, making my way back to the kitchen. Unnerved just a tad, I scurried back to the window, taking another peek out the window. The car was gone. Wringing my hands together, I told myself to pull it together.

"It smells good as shit in her, shorty," Noah complimented.

Blushing, my hand instantly shot up to cover my smile.

"Thank you," I said between my fingers.

The body on this man made me giggle like a schoolgirl, heat shot up my spine back down to the sacred place between my legs. Damn. I mean, shit. I had only been with one man my entire life, but my body suddenly craved for Noah. Slickly, I had admired his muscle tone and fit body whenever he wore a wifebeater and sweats around the house. Tonight was the first time I laid eyes on him without a shirt on, and oh my God, the temptation to lose my salvation was real. The way his third leg was sitting in his grey sweatpants had me salivating. Maybe it was the pregnancy hormones causing my blood pressure to rise.

"Earth to Gianna," he snapped his fingers, raising his eyebrows, wondering where my mind was at.

"I got lost in thought, my bad. Let's eat," I suggested.

We sat at the table discussing our days while eating the shrimp scampi I prepared for us. I didn't want Noah to know who William was exactly, so I was always vague when I spoke about him. Even though I explained our relationship, I advised that I didn't want to give his name or any personal information. Noah respected my privacy, never pushing me to give more than I was willing to. His understanding of my need to keep some things to myself made him that more attractive in my eyes. A part of me wanted to just get it out in the open, but the other part of me didn't want to stain William's reputation. Moving on quickly and quietly would be in the best interest of everyone. Pretending that my husband was just an average joe kept things calm. On Saturdays, even though we checked in with each other, we always went our separate ways. No matter how much I felt the urge to pry deeper into his dating life, I refused. When he left here on Saturday mornings, we never talked about where he was going or what he was doing unless he invited me somewhere.

"This hit the spot, thank you for dinner," he declared.

"Thank you for being great company," I semi-flirted.

"Go relax on the couch while I clean the kitchen," he offered.

"You don't have to tell me twice." I jumped up from the table, giggling.

Settling down on the couch, I fumbled with the remote trying to change the channel. It hit the floor with a thud. Next thing I know, Noah was standing at the edge of the loveseat staring at me like I was crazy.

"You okay?"

"Yes, it was just the remote. I don't know why it made so much noise."

"Ok, I'm almost finished with the dishes. Find us a good Friday night movie."

"I will. Don't be mad if it's girly either."

"Whatever, chump."

Noah lifted my legs, taking a seat on the loveseat, placing my feet down in his lap. He began to massage my toes one by one before moving on to the balls of my feet. By the time he reached the middle of my foot, I moaned so loud, it startled both of us. Never missing a beat, he threw his head back laughing from the pit of his stomach.

"You needed this, huh? All those long hours on your feet every day."

"Mmm-hmm," I groaned. It was all the response I could offer.

"Outside of getting a pedicure, no one has ever rubbed my feet before. I need to make some changes in my life." I sighed as my eyes rolled to the back of my head.

"Your husband never rubbed your feet?"

"He wasn't a feet type of person."

Tapping the bottom of my right foot, he stared at me, bringing my foot close to his face. His lips brushed the middle of my foot, planting a soft kiss directly over my arch. A second kiss followed. I tried to jerk my foot back, but he held it tight. His mouth opened seductively over my big toe. His teeth grazed it gently. Another moan escaped from between my lips.

"Noah, please," I begged.

At that moment, it was unclear to both of us what I was begging for exactly. My mind was firmly set on not crossing a line we could not come back from. My body raging with unbridled passion. If I had been touched properly like a wife should be by William, maybe I'd react differently. Staring at Noah's fine ass, I knew I was lying to myself.

"Please what, Gia? What you want me to do, baby?" he coaxed.

Never taking his eyes from mine, he began to caress my leg, leaving a trail of wet kisses along each place he touched. His hand gripped my thigh, I winced in pleasure. When his warm tongue snaked out of his perfect mouth, licking my inner thigh. I creamed. I knew what was coming next if I allowed it. Clamping my legs shut, I pushed his head up from my body.

"Noah, we can't do this. It isn't right."

"Why ain't it? You're carrying my baby, it's my job to cover all bases in taking care of you. We both know you aren't getting it from anywhere else. And you've been so tense lately. Let me fix that, Gianna," he rasped.

"But, Noah," I whined, covering my face with my hands.

His touch felt like fire traveling at a fast speed down my body. Gently smacking my hands down from my face, he pulled me to him. My belly was in the way, but he managed to fit me in his lap comfortably and just how he wanted me. Now straddling him, my heart was rattling out of my rib cage. Noah's bare chest pressed against my full and heavy breasts, both of us breathing heavy. Placing both hands against his chest, I tried to back away from him. Rather than allowing me to move from his lap, he entangled his fingers in my hair, yanking me back to him.

Our lips collided. I almost sucked his face off, a hunger took over me that I've never felt before. My tongue outlined his lips, his mouth was succulent, he tasted so... him. It wasn't another word for it. Somehow, I knew what he'd taste like, maybe it was from my dreams. My teeth nibbled on his bottom lip until he took control of the kiss, slurping my tongue back into his mouth.

"Noah, we have to stop," I said after catching my breath.

"I want you," he rumbled, the vibration of his voice rattled my chest.

Silence. We stared at one another. His eyes pleading with mine. Mine pleading with him to not make me make this decision. Nothing good would come from this, right? William's adultery was the very reason I was in this position to begin with. The stare-off continued. All in one swift motion, Noah hoisted me off his lap enough to free his bulging manhood. I didn't need to look down at it to know he was working with a monster. The way it pulsed against my body told me everything I needed to know. He ripped my panties off from under my oversized t-shirt, smelling them with a slight smile before flinging them over his head.

Entering two fingers in my throbbing core, my juices leaked down his fingers as I moaned bucking wildly back and forth. When he snatched his fingers out of me, my eyes flew open at the displeasure of him stopping. Slowly, he licked each finger dry, then he gripped both of my hips, bringing me down on top of his dick, inch by glorious inch.

"Ohhh," I cried out.

"Shit," he panted.

My legs buckled once I hit rock bottom on his manhood, my eyes rolled in the back of my head. His hands moved from my hips to my hair, holding me in place, his tongue snaking out to lick my neck.

"You're so wet, mama. That shit is running down my balls."

"Augghhh," was all I managed to say.

Noah bit into the side of my neck, slow and sexy. He began thrusting under me, matching my rhythm. At some point, I lost the power to keep up with him, he felt so good inside me.

"Noah, we have to stop. I don't want to burn in hell," I whimpered.

"Let me take you to heaven first, then you can repent, I promise," he coaxed.

"You promise?" I whined.

"Yes, baby. I promise. I need this pussy, please don't take it from me."

The pounding got deeper and deeper until I exploded all over him, crying out his name. I laid my head on his shoulder, spent and out of breath. Never in my whole marriage had I been fucked like that. William and I always made love slow and tender. Noah just showed me what grown folks do. It made me realize why girls became stalkers, that were getting dope dick.

"You want to repent now or after round two?"

"Round two," I slyly answered.

Chapter Twenty-One

WILLIAM

Bitch Please

"William, I'm sick of this shit!" Sydney screamed in my face.

"Leave then," I shouted.

"You are mine. I don't know why you think you need that stiff, stuck up, bible thumping, soon to be ex-wife of yours by your side. Tonight is the perfect night for us to make our grand entrance as a couple. Baby, it's time to dispel the rumors and the whispers."

"The fucking President of the United States of America is going to show up to my event as the guest of honor. I cannot, I will not show up with anyone other than my wife on my side. Do you know how crazy and unstable I'd look showing up with anyone else? Now is not the time to jeopardize my next step in politics, Syd. Work with me here!"

"All I do is work with you! I am always at your beck and

call. You take advantage of that. I'm growing tired of the nonchalant way you treat me. I love you. Why is it so hard for you to prove to the world how much you love me too?"

"Bitch, I'm a married muthafuckin' man! I'm the mayor! I cannot run around publicly like I am single, and it be okay. You knew this shit, Sydney. So, stop with the dramatics! It's not like you didn't know what you signed up for and what role you'd be playing," I spat, the vein in my forehead about to burst.

"I didn't know I was signing up for HIV, but yet I stayed. I didn't fold. So, who you calling bitch? Your bitch ass can't get enough. Your wife wouldn't have stayed, ain't that her role? Through thick and thin? Well, William, shit has gotten thick! And you running behind her trying to kiss her ass like I ain't the thin. I am the one holding your nasty, I like every type of sex but vanilla ass down. Not once have I complained. But after tonight, things will change. You can count on that shit, buddy. Show up with her on your arm for the public since you feel you don't have a choice. But know I'll singlehandedly ruin your so-called marriage. You think it's in ruins now? Ha!" she threatened. This bitch knew how to push all my damn buttons. At once. It wasn't anyone else on God's green earth that was able to get under my skin like Sydney could.

"Bitch, please!"

"I'll see you tonight at the ball, Mr. Mayor. I might even bring a date. Since I conveniently purchased two tickets," she huffed, spinning on the balls of her feet.

Behind her back, I flipped her the bird. She better not had

shown up to my ball with another nigga. I'd hurt both of their feelings. She was always on some bullshit.

"Aye, don't wear no panties under that dress tonight," I called out to her.

She never looked back to acknowledge me, but I was content with the fact she heard me. Sydney was a certified freak. It was no way she'd let me down on one of the biggest nights of my life.

Once I heard the door slam, my mind went directly to my baby Gianna. Contrary to what people may have thought, I loved Gianna with all of me. There was no one else in this world that I was supposed to be with. It was killing me that she avoided me like the plague, but tonight was the night to change all of that. I even took the liberty to book us a hotel room to retreat to when the ball ended. Cuddling her in my arms all night was the only thing on my heart. I wasn't cleared to have sex with her yet, but that time was coming soon. Inside, I still carried a little resentment of her going out to get pregnant by IVF, but at least she didn't do it the old fashion way. That shit would've torn us apart. Even in moving on, my baby was loyal.

Deciding to take a nap, so I would be well-rested for the evening, I laid across my bed after setting the alarm. The tuxedo was already hanging in the closet, everything else was laid out across my bed like it was the night before the first day of school. My barber came to give me a fresh cut and line up this morning. No part of my evening had been left up to chance, from the venue down to the watch I was wearing, every single piece was planned out.

I awoke feeling rejuvenated, it was almost showtime. It wasn't a word to describe the way I felt. If I was a less confident man, I'd be nervous. However, I was William Wesley, the great. The only mayor in the history of Ohio to not only have the balls to invite the President of the United States but the only one a president had ever shown up for. I was that dude—no two ways about it. With Gianna on my arm, I was unstoppable. My only problem was all night I knew I'd have to accept congratulations about a baby I didn't father. But with her being in her sixth month, it wasn't a possibility of hiding her belly. Her parents kept me updated from afar with the progress of the pregnancy.

My phone dinged, alerting me that I had a message. Scanning the message, my mood picked up even more when I read the text. My right-hand man had the information on the little nigga that I needed Jared to take care of for me. This day kept getting better and better. I'd pull Jared aside this evening while the party was in full swing to give him the drop on the dude. Even though Jared didn't exactly commit to murkin' the dude, I was sure he'd make it happen. The wild part was I respected the hell out of Jared more than any of the other dudes I forced to the other parts of town. Jared was all business, all the time.

A call came in from Pastor Baxter, he wanted to confirm the time the limo would be arriving. We chatted a while about Gianna finally giving in this evening. Both of us praying that she came to her senses about coming home to me. The world of fame I was destined to step into after tonight, was a world she should be proud of. Her husband, the mayor, the future governor, maybe the future president if I played my cards right. In politics, it wasn't always what you knew but instead who you knew.

My mom said when I grew up, I could be anything in the world I wanted to be. She believed in me like no other, I knew she was looking down on me from heaven with a special smile, hand over her heart mouthing "my son." Whenever I allowed my mind to wander to my mom, my heart filled with love. She was an amazing woman. It saddened me to think of how she died after having a heart attack one day at work. My father wasn't shit to me. I remembered all the times he told my mother I wasn't going to amount to nothing but a con artist. The joke was on him. What grown ass man tells his son he won't be shit? But look at me now, I'm the man. If it wasn't for my ego, him, his new wife and family would've been invited to my big night. However, he needed to see his con artist son rub shoulders with the highest power in the land. It was time for me to start getting ready, here comes the magic!

Chapter Twenty-Two

CHANTEL

The Mayor's Ball

*E*merald green and gold were the colors that Jared and I chose to wear for the Mayor's Ball. My dress was the classier version of Jessica Rabbit's dress from the movie

"Who Framed Roger Rabbit." The dress was green instead of red, and the split hit my thigh in a respectable place. My accessories were gold, my shoes were chunky heel peep-toe heels. Jared purchased me a brown mink shawl for my shoulders to complete the outfit. Earlier that day I had my hair done in a half up, half down curly ponytail. My face was beat to the gawds and I smelled delectable. I was feeling myself tonight.

Jared's hands were trembling when he was trying to get his bowtie on correctly. It's rare to ever catch Jared nervous, I wondered what was going on with him.

"You good, babe?"

"Yes, just want this damn bow tie to be on straight. Tonight is important. I don't want anything to go wrong," he said, his voice trailing off at the end.

"I've never seen you so handsome, babe. I might need to carry some sneakers and Vaseline to be ready to beat these thirsty hoes off you," I flirted.

"Fuck them hoes. Ain't nobody better than you, bae."

Jared was looking so dapper in his tux, it crossed my mind to say fuck it let's keep this on and create our own magic here at the house. But I knew this would be a once in a lifetime event, so that thought fled my mind as quickly as it came. Plus, his parents, Noah and my mother were all waiting on us to pick them up in the limo he rented for the night.

"Meet me in the living room when you're done," Jared announced as he left the bedroom with his shoes in his hand.

"Okay, babe. I'll be out in just a few minutes. Let me freshen up my lipstick," I replied.

After I used a toothbrush to lay my baby hair back down in the front, I freshened my lipstick. Grabbing my small gold clutch after making sure I had all the essentials tucked away inside I made my way to meet Jared in the living room. Mr. Roberts whistled as soon as I entered the room.

"Hey, little Ms. Gorgeous. Can I get your number?" he teased.

"Knock it off, that's my woman," Jared bellowed in a fake deep voice.

We all started laughing at the same time. Everyone was

here. Giving everyone the once over, I had to admit we were one good looking bunch. Seeing Noah standing there alone hurt a little. Alana had really fucked up. I wish things had turned out differently, but Alana made her bed and had to lay in it.

"Can I sit with y'all? Out here looking all grown and sexy," I catcalled.

My mother did a twirl, showing her ruby red long sleeve, off the shoulder, form fitting mermaid dress. It seemed my mother never aged. She still could pass for about thirty when really, she was almost sixty. Being that I still got carded everywhere I went, I knew that she passed those good genes to me. That I was happy for, but hey, you know what they say. Black don't crack. The clan all thanked me individually, primping around in their ensembles.

"I thought we were picking you guys up?"

"We decided to meet here instead. Have a glass of champagne with y'all before we got the night started," Noah explained.

We could have had a glass of champagne in the limo, I thought. However, I didn't speak on it out loud. I had planned to get as close to sex in the rear of the limo as possible with Jared on the way to pick up his parents. The excitement was high in the air, so I didn't want to mess up the vibe. The whole family seemed to be on pins and needles. Yes, we'd meet the President tonight, but shit, his ass was human just like the rest of us.

"Help me get the champagne for us," Jared said to Noah.

"You got it, bro," he answered with a grin.

I figured we'd be here another hour or so since we didn't have to make any stops on the way to the event. Unstrapping my shoes, I kicked them off, deciding not to ruin my feet before the night got started. I planned to dance the night away with Jared. Well, maybe Noah because Jared only had a couple songs in him with a good two-step. Taking a seat in Jared's favorite wingback chair, I grabbed the remote to turn on the fireplace.

"Chan, come out to the dining room so we can toast, babe," Jared called to me.

Easing up from the chair, I huffed. I hadn't even noticed that I was all alone in the living room. I thought they were still behind me, just standing around. Music came through the speakers in the house, it was an old R&B song that I knew my mother or his mother put on. They always had to have an oldie on. Listening to the words trying to pick up the song to determine if I knew it, I realized it was *Never* by umm what is his name? Jaheim. Waltzing into the dining room, I was dramatically singing the words. I twirled when I reached the entrance of the dining room, eyes closed, singing my heart out.

"Chantel."

"Neverrrrrrrrrr," I sang, opening my eyes.

My head jerked back in shock when I noticed Jared on the floor kneeling in the frame of the entrance on one knee. When he opened the little blue box, all the wind was knocked out of my body. I felt faint. My nerves were shot, my brain buzzing with racing thoughts. Was any of this real? I pinched my wrist to be sure this wasn't a dream, the room erupted in laughter. It was real.

"Chantel Mann, will you do me the honor of being my wife?" Jared proposed.

Tears streamed down my face, clouding my vision as I scanned the room, looking into the faces of our family that surrounded us. This was love, this was the dream, this was my life, and this was real.

Barely getting out the words, I choked, "Yes! Yes! Yes! A million times yes, Jared, I will marry you!"

The whole room erupted in celebratory screams as Jared slid the ring on my finger. The diamond was blinding; canary was my new favorite color. Balloons floated down over us, and a string of lights lit up that I'd never seen before. It was a perfect beginning to the rest of my life. How they managed to set this up without me knowing was baffling. Jared picked me up, squeezing me tight in his strong arms. Flooding my face with kisses, he whispered all types of sweet nothings in my ear.

I whispered back, "Baby, put me down before you start something in here in front of our family."

Chapter Twenty-Three

NOAH

What The Hell

The line was long, but it was moving. The extra added security was understandable since the President would be in attendance. Our limo dropped us off in front of the building, letting us know he'd wait in the parking lot along with the other limos. He gave Jared his personal cell phone number so he could text him when we were done. The chatter around us mainly consisted of if the President had arrived yet. The anxiety of meeting the President or at least being in the same space as him, blanketed the crowd.

It was amazing how no one seemed to be impatient with waiting to get through security.

*L*ove filled the air. I closely studied the way Jared and Chantel interacted with each other. I've never seen either of them this happy, and it warmed my heart. I was genuinely happy for them. My time for love would come soon. My thoughts traveled to Gianna. It was an unspoken rule that we didn't contact each other on the weekends, but I missed my girl. Last night we took things to another level, making love and repenting for our sins all night until the morning.

We needed to talk. While I was willing to give her time to mourn her marriage, I damn sure wasn't willing to let her go. I made a mental note to text her once we got to our seats. Just to let her know she was on my mind, and still on my tongue. Unconsciously, I licked my lips, still tasting her essence lingering on my tongue. There wasn't an inch on her body that I didn't explore between the night to the morning.

"Are you excited?" Chantel's mother asked me, touching my arm, snapping me out of my flashback from the love I made with Gia.

"Well, I can say I'm grateful for the experience. Are you excited?"

"Damn right, I am! Little ole' me rubbing elbows, not only with the elite of the state but the President. Shit, you could buy me for a penny right now!"

"You are crazy! But I get what you're saying. This is a once in a lifetime type of evening."

"You know, I'd truly thought that you and Alana would be the ones getting engaged, married, and starting a family. Noah, I just want you to know that I love you like a son. Your happiness is important to me, the same way Alana's and Chantel's are. I don't want you to think I'd treat you any less.

Even when you move on, don't forget about me," Ms. Mann whispered to me.

"Ms. Mann, I love you too. Always. You won't get rid of me that easy," I promised.

"Ms. Mann? Boy, I am still Mom to you," she snorted, popping me in the shoulder.

"Sorry, Mom," I apologized, kissing her forehead.

"Next," the security guard ordered.

Jared handed him all of our tickets. They were scanned individually then handed back to Jared. One by one, we were searched by security. We went through metal detectors and were patted down thoroughly by hand. Finally, on the inside, I was blown away on how beautifully decorated this venue was. Wow. I was not a person that was easily impressed, but even I had to admit that this shit was dope as hell. We were escorted to our seats, based on the numbers on the ticket. While I knew Jared was somewhat cool with the mayor, I didn't know they were on like this! We were sat damn near in front of everyone. Our table was a few feet away to the left of the stage where we could see everything. Smooth jazz played through the speaker system, the lady servers were swerving in and out between the tables offering glasses of champagne. The gentlemen servers were weaving the opposite direction of the ladies offering hor d'oeuvres. The way they moved so coordinated, it was quite a sight to see.

Shooting a quick text to Gianna, I told her I missed her. I saw the bubbles come up on my phone to indicate that she was typing, but then it went away. My forehead wrinkled, but

I didn't want to overreact. Maybe she needed to think about what she wanted to say back. Shit, maybe she'll send me a picture. Who knows? She may just need a moment to process what took place between us. No sooner than I placed my phone back in my pocket, I saw the Baxters waltz in the room like they owned it. Their table was just a couple of feet from ours. They took a seat at the table right to the left of us, which was caddy cornered in front us of. Guess they had more pull in the community than I originally thought. Nonetheless, they were the grandparents of my unborn baby. Needing to maintain at the very least a cordial relationship with them, I made it my business to speak.

They returned the greetings to not only me but our whole table. The look of surprise on their faces did not pass me. My eyes swept the room, wondering if Gianna was in the crowd somewhere. Not seeing her, I joined in on the laughter and jokes going on at my table. Our blended family vibe was dope as hell. I hoped nothing would ever change the type of love we all had for each other. My heart still yearned for Alana, but the blow she delivered to my soul was too much for me to bear.

"Hey, this champagne has me needing to find the nearest bathroom. I'll be back, y'all," I told my family.

From the bathroom, I heard the music lower to a barely audible hum. It was a line in front of me, so I hadn't used the bathroom yet when I heard a voice say that someone would be out soon to introduce the President of the United States, then the mayor came out to kick off the rest of the night. My brother texted me to tell me to hurry up. I told him it was about six people ahead of me, but I was coming.

Leaving the bathroom, I went out to the lobby to call Gianna because she still hadn't replied to my text message. I didn't want to pressure her but wanted to make sure she was okay and not having regrets cause I damn sure didn't have any. The lobby was almost empty. Out the corner of my eye, I saw my brother walking towards the mayor. Since I hadn't completed the call to Gianna yet, I started to walk in their direction when I saw Gianna emerge from the ladies' room. She looked stunning, I couldn't tell if she had the pregnancy glow or she was glowing from our lovemaking. Damn, I had to have this woman.

"Gianna," I greeted.

She froze at the sound of my voice.

I heard my brother's voice elevate from the corner he was in with the mayor. He had a manila envelope in his hand. Seeing Gianna's eyes dart between me and them, I didn't quite understand the look of fear on her face. I started towards Jared to make sure he was good, as Gianna dashed out the front doors as fast as she could go. Not understanding what was going on, I decided to follow Gianna because I knew Jared was always good. They didn't call him J-Black for nothing.

"Gia!"

"Gianna!"

"G! Where are you going? What's wrong," I shouted at her back.

The security gates that were set-up caused me to lose her for a minute because I yelled for Jared to bring me my ticket so I could get back in.

When I got outside, she was nowhere in sight. How the hell did she get away that fucking fast? Repeatedly calling her cell phone, I raced back into the building to see if Jared knew what the fuck was going on. Just as I reached Jared, who was pacing back and forth in the lobby, Gianna called me. All I heard was groaning on the other end with heavy breathing, she didn't say anything as I called her name over and over. The line went silent, but she hadn't hung up. I knew instantly something was wrong.

"Jared, I gotta find her, man. Do you know what the fuck just happened? Why she leave like that? What the mayor say to you?" I asked.

Our conversation was drowned out by the loud cheers of the President being introduced, in the ballroom. Jared dropped his head, handing me the envelope that he was gripping on to as he paced the floor.

"Help me," I heard Gianna's voice cry weakly through the phone.

"I'm on my way, baby. Where are you?" I asked, but there was no answer.

"I gotta find her, bruh. She's carrying my baby," I spoke in desperation.

"I have to get the mayor. Hold on, wait right here," he shouted, taking off running.

Moments later, they both came running through the

doors, damn near about to run past me. Confused on why this nigga was with us, I shot Jared a pointed look, but we all jumped in the town car that was on standby for the mayor.

"Niles, did you see which way my wife went?" the mayor asked hurriedly.

"Yes, is everything okay?" he responded.

"No, we have to find her. We think she may be hurt," the mayor answered, shooting me a look of disdain.

"William," my brother threatened without saying another word.

It took my brain a moment to comprehend the word "wife" that fell off the mayor's lips. Massaging the back of my neck with my right hand, I slid the manila envelope from my brother's hand to see what it was he was so angry about. Carefully, I opened the single piece of paper on the inside, there was nothing on it but my name and address. It was at that moment I realized the mayor had put a hit out on my life—this muthafucka. Slowly, I began to ease up from the seat, but Jared snatched my body back. He didn't speak; he just tapped my knee, which I knew that meant for me to chill.

"Is that her car up there on the side of the road?" I pointed out.

Leaping out of the town car while it was still moving, I ran to the car, which was bent all out of shape. My heart skipped a beat because I knew it was her. Hanging up the phone, I dialed 911, but the sounds of their sirens and the fire truck could be heard directly behind me as they got closer. Jared and the mayor caught up to me at the car. The way the door was smashed in, we knew she'd need the jaws of life to pry her out. The other side of the car was rammed up on a bicycle rack that was on the side of the street. Someone had run her off the road and fled the scene. There were no other cars, trucks, or anything else in sight.

"Gianna! Baby, stay with us!" I yelled.

"Baby, it's your husband. I need you. Don't leave me this way," William's cheating ass cried out.

Irritated, I jogged away to see if anyone had seen exactly what happened. No one seemed to know anything, just saw the end of the accident. As the paramedics appeared, I thought I saw Alana in the crowd, but she was gone so quickly I had to have been imagining things.

William called out to someone named Sydney that I guess he knew, but she kept walking by briskly with her head down. Maybe he was seeing things too? What the fuck happened out here tonight?

UNTITLED

TO BE CONTINUED

Bai Jaye

Copyright © 2000 by Steve Lavis. All rights reserved.

Published in the United States by Ragged Bears, Inc.
413 Sixth Avenue, Brooklyn, New York 11215

www.raggedbears.com

Originally published in Great Britain in 1998 by Ragged Bears Publishing
Milborne Wick, Sherborne, Dorset DT9 4PW

CIP Data is available

First American edition. Printed and bound in China.

ISBN 1-929927-11-8

2   4   6   8   10   9   7   5   3   1

Ragged Bears

Brooklyn, New York • Milborne Wick, Dorset

Little Mouse

HAS A PARTY

Steve Lavis

Little Mouse is going to have a party. On **Monday** he gets up early to plan it.

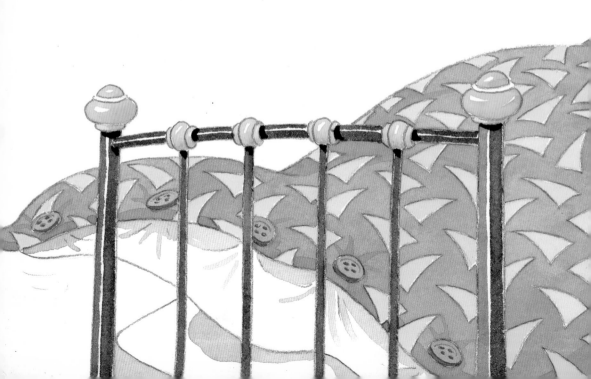

On **Tuesday**
he cleans the house.

On **Wednesday**
he goes shopping.

On **Thursday**
he bakes some cakes.

On **Friday**

he blows up balloons.

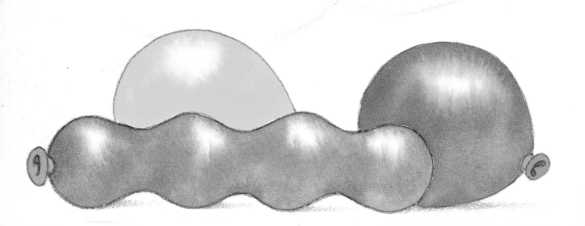

On **Saturday**
he decorates the house.

On **Sunday**
he is ready.
Little Mouse is
having a party...